MW00909749

QUOTES FROM A BUNCH OF PEOPLE
FROM ALL PROFESSIONS
REGARDING STEVEN BRANTNER'S BOOK

◆ ◆ ◆ ◆

*"This book made my wedding possible."*　　　MATT, 27, FARMER

*"I have Steven's book hanging on my refrigerator even though I didn't like it much."*　　　ARLYS, 64, STEVEN'S MOM

*"AMaHW changed my life. I may have even laughed once or twice."*　　　SCOTT, 27, SURGICAL INTERN

*"This is the best book on weddings I've ever made my fiancée read."*　　　BERNADETTE, 35, MARKETING MANAGER

*"I taught Steven how to write like a scholar and all he can come up with is this?"*　　　BARBARA, 51, ENGLISH PROFESSOR

*"It's much better than some boring book by a psychologist."*　　　MARK, 28, PSYCHOLOGIST

*"This is the best wedding book on the market."*　　　ANNE, 28, TEACHER AND STEVEN'S WIFE

*"I don't think I'll ever get married or read a book but if I do either I'd want Steven there with me."*　　　PETER, 25, UNEMPLOYED

# A MAN *and* Her Wedding

# A MAN and Her Wedding

♦ ♦ ♦ ♦

STEVEN BRANTNER

ELTON-WOLF PUBLISHING

Seattle • Vancouver • Los Angeles • Milwaukee • Denver • Portland

ISBN: 1-58619-001-6
Library of Congress Catalog Card Number:  99-65692


First Printing August 1999
Printed in the United States


Published by Elton-Wolf Publishing
Seattle, Washington

ELTON-WOLF PUBLISHING

1101 Alaskan Way Pier 55  Suite 301  Seattle Washington 98101  (206) 748-0345
Email: pnutpub@aol.com   Internet: http://www.pbpublishing.com
Seattle • Vancouver • Los Angeles • Milwaukee • Denver • Portland

*To my dearest Anne,*
*I'm glad I was the man*
*in your wedding.*

# TABLE OF CONTENTS

# ACKNOWLEDGMENTS

I'D LIKE TO LIST THE NAMES OF PEOPLE FROM WHOM I BORROWED STORIES OR RECEIVED ADVICE. *Dr. Scott Anseth*, for being my first editor and getting me on the right track. *Amy Wagner*, for crying when I handed her the manuscript, it was happy. *Dr. Gordon Lell*, for being the best teacher I've ever had. *Bonnie Kam*, my best editor who made me look like a better author than I am. *Beth Farrell*, my publisher and designer, thanks for saying yes when everyone else was saying no. *My mom*, for not liking the book or thinking it was funny but still loving me. *Bernadette, Amy, Craig, Ann, Deb,* and countless other people from ML who supported, encouraged, and helped me along the way. To all my friends and family who actually bought my book even though they are already married or not interested in weddings at all.

Wedding stories taken from the following (you know which ones were yours even though I changed the names to protect the innocent...and guilty): *Skalbeck, Sutmar, Spears, Hasbargen, Donels, Senske, Vagle, Pierce, Hasbargen again, Ayers, Vouk, Pederson, Walstad, Michaels.*

*◆ Preface ◆*

IF YOU'RE READING THIS, IT MAY ALREADY BE TOO LATE. If you're either in the midst of planning a lavish wedding or at least thinking about it, this advice will do no good but here goes: Put this book down and go to Vegas for a quick, easy, and painless wedding! You're still here, huh? If you've already been through the excitement and agony of a wedding and are reading this book to relive the memories, it may prove useful just to make you laugh (or cry). If you like it a lot, please share it with others (not this copy, buy another one and share that). Finally, if you're single and cynical and say that you never want to get married, you may find some good reasons to back those thoughts up.

Well, my whole idea is that if you're going to go through with it, you're going to need some help to survive because, speaking from experience as a man, you're just an accessory. No matter what people tell you, or what you think, it's "her" wedding. Many things in life belong to the man of the house but the wedding, my friend, is not one of them. You will usually be able to call the basement, garage, and maybe even a truck your own. These things can belong to you; they will be a part of you. In the wedding, on the other hand, you are just another accessory like something old, something new or something borrowed. You get the picture. You become something to stand next to the bride and, while you are totally necessary, you're really just along for the ride.

Here's an example to illustrate my point. My wife is a pretty normal and very laid-back woman, if I do say so myself. Even with that being the case, I still catch her saying things like "at *my* wedding, we had..." Only a few moments into your no doubt blissful engagement, you should realize that weddings are planned and controlled almost entirely by women.

To perpetuate this problem, even 99% of the books already on the market are written and edited by women. Now, don't get me wrong, I love women. I even married one. However, men are the hopelessly forgotten gender in this deal and we need help. Not that women push us over and take control all by themselves, there is actually an entire industry, a multi-billion dollar one at that, which happens to cater to women and weddings. There are even wedding "expositions" in convention centers across America. Scary. My only valid point is that men and women need to work together to plan a really excellent wedding, and women have the home court advantage. So this book is my idea of an equalizer.

Last of all, as an introductory remark, I love my wife, our families, and our friends. We were blessed with a very functional family unit, even for the 1990s. Our parents were great to work with and they even picked up most of the bill. However, after saying that, there were still moments of difficulty, disagreement and argument, and there will be moments for you in your wedding planning process and in life as well. With that said, I can now take full rein to mock the members of my family and their pain in dealing with the wedding of March 1997. Along with that, I have attended about 100 weddings (seems more like 1000) in my still young life, and am taking full liberty to mock the ideas of others as well. For those of you who have invited me to your wedding and were unfortunate enough to have me attend, it's nothing personal. I'm just trying to help other people. As everyone knows, the best way to learn is by observing the mistakes of others. I'm here on this earth to share some of these with you from a man's perspective. Don't get me wrong, however: Along with some solid "do nots," I have collected some pretty good ideas as well.

Finally, my disclaimers are over. You'd think I was an attorney or something. Thank goodness I'm not, but I am a reasonably observant and insightful regular guy who had an idea. You see, I want to tell you a little about this book so you can decide whether you want to keep it or not. First, this is not a self-help book. In fact, I was only able to stomach about two chapters of that "Mars and Venus" book so don't worry about me slipping into that. I am not a psychologist or therapist, so don't expect me to change your life. In fact, when I wrote this, I had a painfully boring job at an insurance company that gave me a lot of free time to write. I'm not really an expert on anything, which makes me uniquely qualified to write this book because when most men get married for the first time, they don't have a clue about what they are getting themselves into. These thoughts have been validated by lots of people and should be helpful to you. Thanks for shelling out the dough. I hope you survive your own wedding as a team and I wish you all the best in marriage as well.

*Introduction — Taking the Plunge*

*Scott and Deb had shopped for rings for several months and finally made their purchase in November. Deb was very excited and assumed that she was going to get the proposal and the ring for Christmas that year. Seemed like a fair assumption but it wasn't to be. You see, Scott was more original and devious than that. He wanted to control the situation and he had the upper hand and the ring so he decided to torture Deb for a few months. They loved each other and everything but this was Scott's last chance to be in charge and he was taking it.*

*One time in January, he left a bunch of flight information lying around on the counter in his apartment. Deb took the bait: two tickets to Denver for the weekend. She called her friends immediately and screamed, "This is it! We're going to Denver for the weekend and he's going to ask me!"*

*When she questioned Scott, he said, "Yeah, Dave and I are going out for the weekend to do some skiing. I'll be back Monday night."*

*Every date they had, every night out, every dinner together and every package that was delivered to her house, she was expecting the ring. She was going crazy at this point but then she held a glimmer of hope for Valentine's Day. That must be it. But February 14 came and went with little pomp or circumstance. Finally, on a Thursday night at the beginning of March after a very long day, Scott called Deb at work.*

*"What's going on tonight?" he asked.*

*"Nothing," she responded tiredly. "I was out really late with people from work last night and I just want to sleep."*

*"Yeah, I don't feel like doing anything either, I'll probably just go to bed early too. I'll talk to you tomorrow."*

*With that, he hung up and the setup began. She expected nothing and was content to go home and sleep, but that would not be. Just before she was ready to leave for the day, a bouquet of wild flowers arrived at her desk with a note attached. It simply read, "Meet me downstairs."*

*Now she got a gleam in her eyes and told her friends as she left the building, "Tonight is finally the night!"*

*Indeed it was. Scott was downstairs with a limo, champagne, two new outfits wrapped in gift boxes and, most importantly, the ring. Deb changed on the way to a popular bar where all their friends were waiting to celebrate the engagement. The evening ended in a hotel suite with room service and relief. The moral of the story is: all good things are worth the wait.*

YES, IT ALL STARTS HERE. There's no single greater pressure on a man in the world today than asking a woman to marry him. Wow. That's about all I have to say. Just kidding, I've got about another 100 pages but I digress a lot so don't worry. First, as I go into further explanation in Chapter 8, which is for men only, we are idiots but women are totally irrational. Where does this leave us, you may ask? It leaves us in a position to have to concentrate and do our best to think out of the box. Here's your first shot, the proposal.

In preparation for asking the most important question of your life, you will age about five years. The only thing that you and your fiancée can hope is that the process happens emotionally rather than physically. Either way, it's probably a good thing, just be prepared to get out of shape and grow gray hair out of your ears sooner rather than later. I don't think men who have been through this ordeal will argue much but I'll give you some evidence to back it up.

The high school and college years were pretty great for most men. You could live off your parents, study very little, work even less, and pretty much kick back and relax. Becoming an adult and fiancé is a little different and forces us to be less selfish and more serious. This, on the surface, sounds horrible and for a few Cro-Magnon type men, it probably is. We all knew a few guys who were always the life of the party as the beer-bonging, occasional pot-smoking "Tommy Boy" single guys. But the idea of getting married actually even makes them grow up and get serious because that's the alternative to growing old alone and death.

Now don't get me wrong, the woman you love and get married to should not be an incredibly powerful "fun sucker." Most men will tell you that marrying the woman of their dreams is the best thing that ever happened to them, even if it meant making some different decisions. You can still be the life of the party; it's just that you maybe can't be the life of *every* party anymore. Engagement is your chance to figure out if you're ready for this type of catharsis, so get to work on it.

One problem that men have is that they don't consider the woman's feelings before the big proposal. You could make a fool out of yourself by springing the question on the woman you love without some discussion of the topic. That is not something that a grown-up would do. This is the most important decision of your lives and it would be a good thing to talk about on several occasions before you go for the end zone. This gives you a great opportunity to share your feelings and get everything out in the open so you don't get all hyped up about it and pop the question out of the blue, only to get a blank look and undesirable answer. I mean, this is the new millennium, for crying out loud. Arranged marriages are out of the question and parents don't even need to be consulted anymore, so it comes down to you and the woman you love.

Sure, I know a few guys who went to their love's parents first but what is the point of that? What if they say "no?" Will you abide by their wishes? You shouldn't unless they own their daughter or something and if that's the case, run for the hills and find a woman whose parents aren't missing a few bolts. In any case, for the love of all that's good and pure, please have the talk with her before you take to your knees. On the other hand, don't take all the romance away by ending the discussion with "All in favor of getting married, please respond by saying aye." You can still plan an official proposal for a later date, just please don't make the assumptive close before you've had a chance for discussion.

For me, I'm a hack writer and have very few guts for impromptu gushing, so I had to write it down. For you, maybe you can get out a quick and coherent "Will you marry me?" without totally losing it, but not I. I really advocate spending some time on the proposal and practicing every piece of it several times, just as you would rehearse an important speech at work (especially if you think you need to do some convincing to get her to say yes!) Hopefully, that's not the case, but this is probably the most important speech you'll ever give so you may want to nail it. Lucky for me, I am a Garth Brooks fan and I stole my idea for the proposal from his song entitled "She's Every Woman," which I rewrote and sang to the woman I love:

OUR LOVE
*The laugh of a child, the shine in your eyes*
*A simple touch, a hug, a sigh*
*No matter where we are, it feels like we're alone*
*You are the best that life can be*
*You're all I feel and hear and see*
*Our love is everything that I've ever known.*

*We are the city and the farm*
*So full of fun and full of charm*
*Together is the only place to be*
*Out with our friends late at night*
*When we're alone, I hold you tight*
*We are everything that I want to be.*

*It needs no explanation*
*It's all so clear to me*
*Our love is the destination*
*You and I together will be.*

*Our love will grow as we do too*
*Forever, me and you*
*God will be by our side each and every day*
*Our love is as real as real can be*
*And it's every fantasy*
*Oh, I love you more than I can ever say*
*I love you more than words can ever say.*

Yes, it was mushy and romantic and all that stuff. I sang this song to the woman I love and she cried and said yes twice. It was an incredible reward for having the ring at my house for three weeks, having it burn a hole in my pocket, and having sweat pore from all my orifices like a geyser. Try to beat that! Actually, please don't. Instead, do your best to make the moment a special one by her standards, not yours.

You are correct, I am nuts and a real sap, but you don't have to be Bill Shakespeare to pull this off. I'm certainly not. You should really do your best to make the proposal fit your relationship. If you're adventurous and free-spirited, do it while skydiving but if you're private and quiet, have dinner at home. Don't consider popping the big question in her dorm room when she's standing in a towel. Even if you think that's her dream, I can guarantee you it's not. I know people who did that and, trust me, no one will want to end a storybook like that.

Also, don't ask her in your favorite bar or at a sporting event. I'm not suggesting doing things that aren't "you," just don't do everything that is. I also know a guy who had the whole thing worked out but when they got to that special place, it was raining and he had to pop the question in the car. You just have to roll with it if that happens. At least you tried and that is the whole point.

Here are some pretty good ideas that will make it memorable:

TRY THE COY LEAD-IN WITH THE ACCIDENTAL DISCOVERY TO TRY TO LIGHTEN THE MOMENT:

- Put the ring in a Carmex jar, go hiking or skiing and ask for some Carmex;
- Put the ring in a balloon that's blown up and fill her car or her room with other balloons so she has to pop a bunch of them to find the one with the surprise;
- Put the ring in an Easter basket (Timing is key on this one, as it should be somewhere near Easter);
- Block off the rose garden under Cinderella's Palace at Disney World and put the ring in a glass slipper covered by rose petals;

- If you're crazy and strong, rent a horse and a suit of armor. Ride up to the lady of choice, dismount, grab a knee (being careful of the sword) and ask her to be your Snow White;

- I shouldn't even mention Christmas and the old put it in the stocking deal. It's certainly not creative but it's worked millions of times so have at it.

I'M QUITE PARTIAL TO GEOGRAPHICS:

- Ask her in a significant place, like back at your college campus where you met or at the restaurant where you had your first date. Make sure the woman you love is okay with public displays of emotion. My wife would kill me if I proposed in a public place;

- Go for a hot air balloon ride and, if you're really trying to make it a surprise, try to rig it up so that she thinks she won the balloon ride and doesn't get suspicious;

- Find a place that abounds with natural beauty where you can be alone to share the moment. This was my idea when I popped the question at Gooseberry Falls National Park just north of Duluth, Minnesota.

SOME TOTALLY PUBLIC OPTIONS:

- You could always go with the sky-writer or the PA announcer at a sporting event, or even the jumbo-tron at a concert or game of some kind. Again, this could be embarrassing so be prepared (and be prepared for a negative response just in case);

- Do it on TV. I'll never forget when Ahmad Rashad proposed to Felicia Allen (Bill Cosby's TV wife) on Sunday during the halftime show of some football game. That was pretty impressive.

One last suggestion that will help your engagement go smoothly: Don't let it last for more than 12 months. If you have too much time to mess around, you're going to fall into analysis paralysis and most likely have too much time to change your mind about everything from the cake to the color of your socks. Hopefully, your choice of the person you want to marry will stay set but if you can't get that figured out in one year, it's not going to happen in two. From my perspective, if you can't get it done in 12 months, don't do it! Yes, there are people out there who think they need to be engaged for 10 years, but I think that's insane. One year is long enough to do the work and if you can't set a date right away, you probably shouldn't get engaged anyway.

*♦ Section I: Pre Work ♦*

# 1

♦ ♦ ♦ ♦ ♦

## THE BUDGET

SOMEONE NEEDS TO KEEP CAREFUL TRACK OF THE BUDGET, and since you're a guy and don't know anything about other wedding stuff, I nominate you. If you believe the statistic that money is the number one reason for divorce in America today, you will take the budget quite seriously. Actually, "irreconcilable differences" is the top reason but we all know what that means: Either someone is sleeping around or someone else wants all the money.

No matter who is paying for it, you still need to set and stick to a budget of some kind. Most people set a budget based on the number of guests they plan to invite to the big event. The single biggest expense of the entire deal for most people is the reception and dinner, for obvious reasons. If you have 200 guests and you figure $25 per person using some simple math that even I can do in my head…yes, that's $5,000. The gown is going to be over $1,000 in most cases. The honeymoon may set you back quite a bit as well. Don't forget to include the rings, flowers, music, photography and incidentals.

Yes, you may need to sell a car, get a second or third job, take out a loan, or apply for a scholarship from your family. You are correct, this sounds quite scary and it is. There aren't many young couples who can afford to shell out $10,000 for a wedding, which is about average in this day and age. I've been to a few that probably cost less than $2,000 total and I've also seen weddings that might have pushed $50,000. Again, the important thing is to set a limit and do your damnedest to stick to it. You will have no idea what you're getting yourself into until you sit down and do an estimate of all the things you'll need and slap an average cost on them.

As I said earlier, there are a couple of options: Fund everything yourself or go outside. The most popular method of securing external financing is a parental loan. Our parents are great people and quite generous. They chipped in considerably so we could afford to both have a fantastic wedding *and* buy a home. We realize that we are very lucky and we are quite grateful. However, when accepting money from family, you need to be quite careful that you still maintain decision-making authority. One risk with getting other people intimately involved with planning your wedding is that they will try to micro-manage and start to push their weight around. In most cases, this is not a malicious act, but it can have horrendous consequences.

Honestly, if accepting money from our parents would have meant giving up our executive privileges, I may have thought twice. You need to follow your heart on that one, but be brutally honest and careful at the very beginning and it will work out. For example, let's say the parents volunteer to pick up the dinner at the reception or the honeymoon. That's a nice gesture but my parents and in-laws have different tastes than my wife and I. For example, my in-laws might have chosen Chinese food, which I hate, no offense to China, and my parents would have sent us on a honeymoon to Branson, Missouri, which my wife hates, no offense to the Osmonds. You get the picture. Make your own decisions.

When it comes to funding the whole thing on your own, you need to be even more careful because creating deep debt by overdoing your wedding will put a lot of undue stress on your already fragile new marriage. This is probably not new information to you, but there is a huge temptation to go crazy because it sounds like so much fun. Also, remember that women are totally irrational when it comes to the wedding so you will more than likely be on your own when it comes to cutting back.

On the positive side, this is a great time to work together on money for the first time and come up with a plan to make it work. There are a lot of resources out there on the market that will help you save money on your wedding and even though I make some suggestions throughout, that's not my specialty. Again, I still believe that weddings can be a team sport and that it's possible to make a deal that ensures this. As a result of being clueless about most things in this process (flowers, dishes, dresses, etc.), you should volunteer to handle the finances. This will give you a useful role and allow you to establish some accountability as well. If you stink at managing money, too, then you should call the whole thing off because you'll be even more useless as a spouse than you are as a fiancé.

# 2

◆ ◆ ◆ ◆ ◆

## WEDDING COORDINATORS

*Wade and Laura were the victims of parents with too much money
and too little common sense, which is quite common. Laura's parents actually circumvented the bride and groom and proceeded to
hire a coordinator and spend $100,000 on the wedding. Every detail
was produced by a creative design firm, including creating paper for
the invites and programs and picking silk window treatments for the
reception that matched the chosen colors. The coordinator even chose
the wedding gown, a very personal choice by most brides. Laura's
only involvement was being measured. The bride and groom were
introduced to the coordinator on the wedding day and each and every component of the day was a surprise to them. It all sounds a bit
fairy tale-ish, which may be fine for children and Disney but not life.
Moral of the story: go with the arranged marriage before you go
with the arranged wedding.*

WHILE THAT MAY BE A BIT DRAMATIC, wedding coordinators may
nonetheless blow your wedding out of proportion and run away with
all the money. They are just like any other consultants in business
and, worst of all, they are 99% women. This means they will prey
upon your ignorance and feed your fiancée's irrationality. If you use
the excuse that "We're too busy to plan our own wedding," I say,
"You're too busy to get married." This is a complicated and important event. If you are committed to it and even the least bit organized, it isn't a problem to handle everything yourself. Seriously, if
you can't seem to handle it, for crying out loud, please elope to Las
Vegas and get married by Elvis. Call me and I'll come down and be a
witness, or better yet, you can pay me to be a consultant.

Honestly, there were people who tried to talk us into using a coordinator, but I wouldn't stand for it. I saw the Steve Martin version of "Father of the Bride" a few months before we were engaged and I vowed that no one named "Franc" (pronounced like the former French currency) would ever be able to talk me into having real swans walking around at my wedding. On the other hand, there are infinitely too many details to take care of completely on your own, but that doesn't mean the answer is to throw everything over to someone else.

To stay sane, there are some easy things that you can do. First, most churches, hotels, and country clubs have coordinators on staff who can assist you with some of the details. These people are usually included in the price of the facilities and are very helpful members of your team. Use them to answer questions and to work with other vendors like DJs, florists, caterers, and the like so that everyone shows up at the right time and gets things done.

Also, there will be many people in your life to whom you can easily delegate tasks. This is the oldest and best trick in the book. You need to become a vice-president who does nothing but hand out tasks for others to do. I know people like this (remember, I worked in the insurance industry). You and your bride have the vision and you are going to need help pulling it off, so use your friends and family who are dumb enough to offer their assistance.

Here are a few examples. My parents took care of the hotel arrangements for my extended family and gave a lot of great advice because they had survived the weddings of my siblings. They were great. My in-laws helped with tons of stuff, including booking a limo, finding musicians, licking and sticking all the invitations, and collecting the RSVP's. They were awesome. A neighbor of my wife's family owns a flower shop and she was fantastic with the flowers and providing other decorating tips. You will have friends who volunteer, so put them to work. We had friends do photos at our reception, coordinate the tuxedo rental process with the guys, and help pick out the wedding gown, so I didn't have to be involved at all.

One final note on caving in: I have never known anyone who needed to hire a wedding coordinator to set the whole deal up. However, I'm sure there are some great ones out there who could really help you so I'm not going to rule it out completely. Just do me a favor and make sure you know what you're getting yourself into. After all, if you have about 12 months to plan, are even slightly organized, know how to make some lists, and can delegate effectively, you can probably pull it off all by yourself. This may be another role for you as the guy: Volunteer to make lists and/or delegate some tasks to others. This is a great and very important role and your future wife will appreciate it beyond all measure. Adding value is key and, again, since you are not qualified to make any decisions, volunteer to handle some of the administration and management duties.

# 3

• • • • •

## THE RINGS—
## DON'T BREAK THE BANK

*Jim was a man's man, a strapping, 6' 3", 265-pound former college football star. He exemplified the "bull in a china shop" analogy as he stepped into the mall jewelry store. This was his first trip to look at diamonds and he was clueless, unfortunately for him and his fiancée, Carrie. So was the salesman who preyed on him.*

*Don't get me wrong. Jim was no moron, just quite a few miles out of his element and out-talked a bit by "Slick Willie" from Diamonds-R-Us. He did the right thing by spending three months' salary but the wrong thing by not consulting Carrie to learn her preferences. When the big day came, Carrie said yes and accepted the ring but it wasn't at all like the one in her dreams. Moral of the story: learn her dreams and help them come true, even if you don't get it at all.*

Yes, diamonds are forever, but so is the debt for overachievers. This idea about three months of salary for an engagement ring is a tradition that has overstayed its welcome. As my dad would say, "You can't eat a diamond," and if you put it on a list of the most important things in life, it shouldn't even make the top 1000. I'll explain the whole diamond thing to you in a couple of cheap pages. I'm not spending much time on this issue because you've probably already been suckered into a big old diamond for the engagement. Sorry I didn't get to you sooner; the guy at the mall probably ripped you off. Jewelers can be just as difficult as used car dealers and there's no easy way to check the quality of their merchandise. As with everything else, try to get a referral from family or friends to help narrow down your options.

One quick thought on the process. I'm not sure how thrilled the object of your affection is with surprises, but I wouldn't suggest making the ring your first experiment. Women, and I mean all women, know exactly what kind of ring they want by age six. They also have very distinct opinions on the rings they *don't* want, so if you screw that up, you're in big trouble. Here's a way to make it work. After you've been seriously involved to the point where love has been mentioned several times, start allowing yourself to be dragged into jewelry stores to look at engagement rings. Don't make a big deal out of it. Just put yourself in a position to let that happen and roll with it.

Do your best to ask questions about styles and observe her reaction to the ones she tries on. Now, for me, I didn't want to take any chances with this decision, so I made her actually pick out the exact style she wanted. It happened to be a very simple solitaire setting with a single diamond, but there are many options and you need to follow her lead. You can still spring the timing on her and make it somewhat of a surprise, but don't go out on a limb and pick everything out yourself, unless you are either some kind of genius or an incredible idiot.

On a serious note, because a diamond is forever and also quite beautiful, it's by that nature very complicated as well. For the same reason that you shop around for cars and check the "Blue Book" value, you should do some homework on diamonds. My suggestion is for you to go to a few places and ask similar questions. See if you get similar answers. If not, check jewelers against each other. It's only fair, after all. If you were going to buy a car, you would take it for a drive. In this situation, you're buying a small piece of compressed coal and that's all you're going to end up with if you're not careful.

You will hear a lot about the "3 C's: cut, color, and clarity." These items are rated on scales and the more you spend, the purer the stone in all categories. Also, each diamond has its share of blemishes, so make sure you ask to see the problems with each of the stones you inspect. If your jeweler says that your stone is perfect, either he is lying or you're in big trouble for getting the world's smallest diamond. Ask to see prospective stones under a microscope or one of those dopey-looking jeweler lenses that fit on one eye. It only makes sense to see the stones you're considering with these tools. A good jeweler won't refuse. They just don't get asked very often.

With the actual wedding bands, I may be in time to be helpful. The tradition is for the bride and groom to wear matching gold bands. The circle symbolizes the undying love that you are both committing to as you take your vows. Stick with that. Don't get talked into some ridiculous baguettes or gaudy diamond chips. If you're going to get ripped off with a diamond solitaire, don't let some sweet-talking jeweler or your fiancée talk you into whoring it up with a bunch of other stuff on the side, too. For your wedding band, please keep it simple. She may try to pick it out, but don't let her get you something that the guys will laugh at. An attractive bevel cut around the outside of the gold is a great look and platinum, though expensive, is attractive for men as well. To reiterate, unless you want to look like a rapper or professional athlete (it's amazing and sickening that they have become so similar), pick out some plain and moderately-priced styles. Also, clearly indicate your preferences and if possible, pick out the band yourself so you know what you're getting into.

# 4

• • • • •

## THE PEOPLE–PICK THE BEST!

*The best man has a key role in this whole process. He is usually called upon to hold the ring until the appropriate time in the ceremony. Speaking of the rings, I believe that they are the most important props of the day. Jake didn't take this very seriously from the very first time that his best friend, Larry, asked him to be the best man. Jake continuously joked about losing the ring and said things like, "How much is the ring worth anyway? I hope I don't have a hole in my pocket or something," and "I promise I won't go to the can and accidentally flush it (the ring) down the toilet."*

*People laughed the first few hundred times, but after awhile it wasn't funny. That didn't stop Jake, however. He persisted with the comments about his irresponsibility up until the wedding day. You guessed it: Destiny was at the wedding that day but the all-important ring was no where to be found after Larry gave it to Jake. The pastor spoke those all-important words in his best soft church voice, "Do you have the ring?"*

*Larry looked at Jake a little nervously but knew he had given it to him only a few minutes earlier. Jake started digging through his pockets, and humor turned into panic. The guests sensed it and broke out into nervous laughter. Julie, the bride, started crying and the rest of the bridesmaids chimed in. Thankfully, one of the groomsmen was married and he quickly stripped his wedding band off his own hand and headed for Larry. The ceremony went on and Julie and Larry were announced as man and wife but they never found the ring. Needless to say, Jake will not be chosen as a best man again anytime soon. The moral of the story is: choose wisely.*

Wᴇᴅᴅɪɴɢs ᴄᴀᴜsᴇ ʜᴜɢᴇ ᴘʀᴏʙʟᴇᴍs ᴡɪᴛʜ sᴏᴍᴇ ᴘᴇᴏᴘʟᴇ, and it can make you (the bride and groom, the only people who really matter) feel terrible. This is very unfortunate, but there are a few ways to get around the potential problems. Picking the correct woman is a pretty big deal but I spend quite a bit of time on that in Chapter 7. As I expand on later, you should marry a woman you love, but you should also find one who has mental health in her family. If your family is anything like mine (big and weird), you'll need all the normal genes you can get.

Seriously, at some point, you will *really* get to know your wife's family but that might be several years down the road and too late to run for the hills. As a result, it may be in your best interests to antagonize your future in-laws before you say "I do." Some quick ideas to get the job done:

- Insult your fiancée in front of them to see if they come to her defense. If, after you make some snide comments, they move in for the kill, that's *not* a good sign;
- Take a look at family albums. Check for obvious things like participation in skinhead rallies, portraits in front of the Confederate flag, or relatives who don't stand fully upright;
- Snoop in the garage and/or basement for things like "Perot for President" or "Ventura for Governor" signs, secret bomb shelters, or an arsenal of assault weapons and camouflage gear.

I think you get the picture. If you do this basic research, you will know what you're getting yourself into.

After you feel moderately confident with the emotional and psychological well-being of your future in-laws, tackle the invitation list. You've got to stop somewhere for several reasons, but I'll give you the best reasons to include and exclude people. Pick a number based on your budget and stick to that number no matter what. Now if you can get this done better than we did, I applaud you. We invited too many people who I didn't want on the list but that's life and we survived. Technically, you should be able to hold a wedding in your back yard or the courthouse because you only legally need two witnesses. The day ends up being so busy that you can't really talk to more than about 20 people, no matter how hard you try, so let the other 200 stay home. We had about 200 people that showed for our big day, and I know I only spent time talking to about half of them. I felt really bad because one of my friends came all the way from Iowa with his wife and daughter and all I had time for was, "Hello, how's it going?" and "Goodbye." That was a total bummer.

A good rule to use is holding the list to people you have talked to in person or corresponded with by phone or mail in the last 12 months. This should definitely include all of your closest friends and relatives. If not, you probably don't need to invite them at all. If it were up to me, we wouldn't have invited as many distant relatives and friends of our parents, but then that's not totally fair either. I was able to cut about 100 of my closest cousins because either I've never met them or they weren't going to come from Sticksville, Utah anyway. A wedding becomes a family event and parents tend to get a little excited. Besides, they deserve a celebration because they are old and finally getting rid of one of their kids. So, you need to allow them to invite a few of their friends and favorite relatives, even though you don't know any of those people.

When it comes to attendants, most brides and grooms face one of their toughest decisions. In fact, you may even lose friends and seriously upset your family over it. My thinking is that if you lose friends/family over an issue like special jobs in your wedding, good riddance to them. Yes, that is exceedingly harsh, but it's incredibly ridiculous to let the petty selfishness of some people get in the way of your special day. Both my wife and I had to exclude people from our wedding party who had chosen us to be in theirs. That was awkward, but definitely the right decision. I actually lost a friend over this but I've moved on. In reality, I saved us both some time and energy because it wasn't going to last anyway. Bygones. Let them be.

The strategy is similar to that of the invitation list. You need to make some cuts somewhere and they may be difficult, but you need to do what's best for you. For both my wife and I, we had to come up with a way to shorten our list of bridesmaids/groomsmen, and it involved cutting people for whom we had served in similar capacities. When you hold it up to the grand scheme of things, it's not that big of a deal. After all, people change and move on and get new friends. Don't feel bad about excluding people, it may be a blessing in disguise. Maybe they didn't want to rent a tux or buy a hideous dress for one night anyway. The most important thing to do is make sure you're happy. Don't exclude people who you really want to be a part of your day, but don't make exceptions based strictly on the "I was/was not in their wedding" principle either.

Men, here's another role for you. Women have a much more difficult time than we do with the guest list. So do your best to help by cutting out friends of your fiancée who you dislike. I actually did this and it was lots of fun for me. I got to make our wedding a better place to live by excluding a moron, which helped my wife and made her feel better. If she had to, she could have actually blamed it on me, but it wasn't a problem and it worked out well.

One other thought on this is to go with family over friends in the top positions. From my perspective, you are stuck with family for your whole life. Now maybe I'm just a nerd, but I don't have many friends who I have known for 27 years. Also, if your family is like mine, you probably need a good reason to get everyone together because life is pretty busy. You make the call that's best for the team. Also, there are some creative ideas out there for the best man and maid of honor, too. I've seen some couples who made a tough situation work. One guy picked his only sister as the best "man" and his wife picked her only brother as "maid" of honor. Don't worry; there was no cross-dressing. It was just a good way to make all the friends finish second so there were fewer hard feelings.

Ushers have a key role at most weddings because they become traffic cops and end up being the "go to" people who handle a lot of key stuff at game time. Contrary to popular belief, you have some gender flexibility for choosing ushers. I've ushered several times and was also part of a mixed gender usher party at a friend's wedding that ended up working quite well. As I see it, ushers are usually the friends of the groom who end up showing people to their seats during the ceremony. However, don't be too quick to pick a bunch of putzes because they need to be quite responsible and able to handle some tricky last minute stuff. Ushers have a much tougher job than your average groomsman/bridesmaid because they don't get to just stand around and walk down the aisle. Ushers are the working class. They get stuck doing all the important stuff and then end up getting stiffed for the head table. That's America for you.

This brings me to ring bearers and flower girls. This is a very tricky decision so listen up. Your wife or mom or sister may try to talk you into allowing some cute little kids to walk up and down the aisle during the ceremony. However, as the voice of reason, you may have to step in and cut this idea off at the short little knees. Little kids are always very cute all dressed up in pint-sized tuxedos or poofy dresses but they are also very difficult to manage. Children are like a force of nature that you can't control, only hope to contain. For that reason, there are a couple of quick things to think about when you are considering using child labor.

First, never choose a child who is too young to reason with. For example, if the kid is under school age, you may not be able to get them to understand their role and pull it off during crunch time. Four-year-olds are cute and all but when they see a church full of people they may refuse to walk down the aisle or even worse, they may run down screaming for their mommy. Not a good scene for the most beautiful day of your life. Next, if you find a responsible kid to carry out your plan, make sure that their role is very simple and has an out at the end. For the ring bearer, let the little person walk down the aisle with a container or something. I suggest not giving them the actual ring. Let me again remind you that the ring is the most impor-tant prop of the day and kids may lose it or refuse to give it to you at the appointed time. I don't think you want to chase a little kid around to get the ring while your guests laugh hysterically.

We gave my nephews two little ring boxes to carry and filled them with candy to eat when they were finished. Also, always let kids sit down in the front row instead of making them stand up in the front during the whole ceremony. They may steal the show by walking around, sitting down, or pulling their dresses up over their heads.

The human shield is an idea that I wasn't able to pull off because I'm a control-freak perfectionist but I got the advice from a few people so I thought I'd pass it on anyway. If you just had a wedding, are in the middle of wedding plans, or thinking about them, you know how many details there are. Now, I'd like to take you to a point in time and have you picture it. Think of the most important day of your life, and think of the busiest time of your life. Now combine those two and you're on the wedding day. The human shield is really the ingenious act of delegation. Nothing more to say! Just kidding, I've got a few chapters left.

Here's a tip though: For you and the bride to remain sane and really be able to enjoy your own wedding, you need to limit your involvement in last minute decisions and actions. Each of you need to pick one person, maybe the best man and maid/matron of honor, a trusted usher, or even better, a couple people you really trust who aren't in the wedding, and delegate all decisions and actions as of the start of the rehearsal to them. You may think this sounds unnecessary now but I can assure you that it's not.

The old adage that says "It's not *if* something is going to wrong, it's *when* it will happen" does apply to weddings, as well as the rest of life. If you've done your planning and everything in your power to make things turn out great, the rehearsal dinner is the time to let go of the reins, relax and enjoy yourself. There's no halfway on this one, either. You need to instruct everyone who comes up to you or your bride with a question or concern to go find your "shield" and lay it on them instead.

Trust me, this will take much of the burden off you and ensure that you enjoy yourself on your special day. Besides, there's nothing else you can do at that point anyway. For me, it's like having to correct your own tests in elementary school, which I hated doing. You have to sit there and evaluate your own mistakes or rethink decisions when it's too late to change. Forget it. Set the flight plan, go on autopilot, and defer all questions to other people. It may be too much to pull this off, but you could consider being the shield for your bride on the big day as well. This role may be easy for you, since you may have less riding on some of the decisions as a result of having less of a part in making them. An offer to lead the problem-solving team for your bride will take many burdens off her shoulders and she will be very thankful.

# 5

◆ ◆ ◆ ◆ ◆

## THE DATE

No, I'M NOT TALKING ABOUT THAT REALLY UNCOMFORTABLE EVENT when you first met (although this date will sometimes seem just as awkward and ridiculous). I am, of course, making reference to the date of the wedding. Oh yeah, there are so many countless other ridiculous things going on that you may forget that you need to agree on a date with what seems like the entire hemisphere.

Here's a very important tip–pick the date that works best for you (bride and groom) and tell everyone else to take a long walk off a short pier. Pardon the harshness, but I have to get tough on this one. I know your mom always taught you to be thoughtful and never selfish and Robert Fulghum made a bundle of dough reminding us that all we ever needed to know we learned in kindergarten. That's all nonsense when it comes to your wedding. Be selfish; it may be the only chance you ever get. Trust me.

If you don't follow this rule, here's how it will break down, and I'm not kidding, either. My wife and I struggled a little to pick a date that was best for us. We came up with March 22, the first day of my wife's spring break from teaching fifth grade. This would allow us to take a honeymoon immediately following the wedding and branch out a little from the typical June wedding. We were quite excited and that was our first mistake. My mom freaked out and said, "March is the absolute worst month for blizzards, the family will never make it down there."

My wife's mom said, "The first day of spring break will never work because all of our friends will be going out of town." The photographer was not available and the really pretty spring flowers were not blooming yet. This is only the beginning. It was also the birthday of one of our best friends, the day of a huge semifinal NCAA men's basketball game, the day before Palm Sunday, and the wedding day of some cousin I hardly knew. All these other things don't matter and all you have to do is say three simple words to whoever/whatever is telling you that your date won't work: "We don't care!"

This is another perfect example of a situation where you may need to step in and help with a decision because your more emotional half may feel bad about being selfish. Here's your chance to do something that you're good at. Men are by nature more selfish than women, so go with that. In actuality, you may want to dial it back just a bit from my hard line, but the point is to do what works best for you in this situation. Everyone will have a different suggestion and just like the old cliché says, "You can't please everyone all of the time." Because of that, just make sure you do what's best for the two of you.

# 6

• • • • •

## To Live or Not to Live, Together?

*Kari and Dave lived together for about four months before marriage. Both were living with friends about 25 minutes away from each other. This was not terribly convenient, but living together on purpose was never an option. However, they started looking at homes the fall before the wedding. The realtor suggested getting pre-approved to be ready in case they found something they liked. They looked at several places in their price range; some were crummy, some had idiots for neighbors, and then there was a great place that seemed perfect. An offer was made and the next thing you know, Kari and Dave were homeowners.*

*This was kind of scary because they were both in leases with friends and didn't really know what to do. So, Dave gave two months notice and found someone to take his place at his old house. Kari and her roommate didn't renew their lease for another full term. Dave moved in to the new place in January and Kari's stuff started coming in a couple months later. She stayed at her apartment until her lease ran out, but when it did, they were living "in sin," as they call it in the Bible belt. However, they made a decision to save the ultimate oneness for the honeymoon, but as irony would have it, no one believed them when they told the truth. It actually turned out to be quite convenient for putting the finishing touches on the wedding because they were in the same place all the time. Moral of the story: be an adult and do what's best for you.*

To live or not to live; that is the question, whether 'tis nobler…sorry, I slipped into Shakespeare for a moment. No, this is not a chapter on the meaning of life or how to live longer by eating your vegetables. I'm talking about that age-old question that gives your grandparents fits and the neighbors something fun to talk about: Should you live together before you're married? Wow, the mostly light-hearted and humorous book stumbles into questions and answers of morality. Don't worry, this and my thoughts on love are as far as I will take it. I refuse to talk about abortion or the President's sex life or legalization of marijuana either (in this book anyway), but if you're interested in these topics, give me a call sometime.

As you walk down the path of life, you may have several room-mates. In fact, I hope you do. It builds character and enhances per-sonal growth to learn how to live with other people. This is a lifelong skill that you couldn't have possibly learned in kindergarten, sorry again, Robert Fulghum, but not only were you wrong, but also clueless. Anyway, the question I'm addressing today is whether you should you make your fiancée your roommate before it's official. Here's the answer, and I'm sorry that it sounds like something your parents said when you asked for a pony or cable TV: maybe. Actu-ally, in most situations, my answer is yes, but I know that Jerry Falwell and the rest of the moral majority (oxymoron) will picket outside my home if I go all the way so I have to make a partially lame case for "maybe" instead.

We had some friends whose parents are the Flanders from the Simpsons, and they had to pretend they weren't sleeping together before the wedding. I don't even think you're allowed to sleep to-gether when you are married in their eyes. Anyway, they actually moved their wedding date up several months so they wouldn't have to live separately and continue lying to everyone. Now that's deter-mination (and horniness), I guess. There were still other friends who went out of their way to make it complicated. She had an apartment with another female roommate just to make it look good and he had a studio apartment of his own as well. Unfortunately, he only spent the night in his studio about six times in eight months and the two of them and their secret cohabitation drove her roommate crazy. To me, this is paying double rent to fool your parents, which I cannot sup-port. Why don't you just live together and spend the extra rent money on prophylactics and charitable organizations that support illegitimate children? Enough blabbing about our former friends, who may now hate us, but freedom of speech is more important than covering up fibs. Besides, it's not like I used their names or anything.

On another note, if you need to keep it separated to keep your parents happy and keep them financially committed to the wedding, go for it. This is quite admirable in my book, but since this *is* my book, I think it's quite stupid as well. It seems like a very childish way to solve an adult problem. If you're 16 and you're running off to live with and marry your math teacher, you're a moron and you should listen to your parents. Likewise, if you and the person you love decide as a couple that you don't believe in living and/or sleeping together before the wedding, that's great. I support that 100%. Just don't try to fool the entire world with some big public game of "We have separate addresses and we're not having sleep-overs, either." Remember that your parents, no matter how old and goofy they are now, were young and in your shoes once.

If you decide as a couple that it's something you want to do, please go ahead and do it. You have my blessing. A lot of social scientists have wasted thousands of hours of research and killed millions of trees trying to solve the problem, "Does living together before marriage help or harm a relationship?" I have the answer. If people would actually get married for the correct reasons, it wouldn't make any difference where they slept on the night or months prior to the wedding. It's worked out both ways and it will continue to be such. The secret to a happy marriage is not whether or not you live together first; it's whether or not you learn to work together first. Do that and you'll be set, no matter what. No, I'm not giving a money back guarantee if it doesn't work out! Good luck and God bless.

# 7

* * * * *

## LOVE–IT IS THE KEY!

*Ben and Liz were very much in love and had their wedding all set.*
*They had survived all the planning and were only a few days away*
*from pulling it off in Liz's hometown. Liz headed for home on Tues-*
*day but Ben got delayed a few days to close out a few things at work.*
*As Ben traveled, he ran into a few roadblocks and met Amy. Amy*
*was a woman like no other Ben had ever known. She was wild and*
*crazy and Ben was instantly attracted to her. This threw a wrench in*
*the "happily-ever after" deal and his honest pre-wedding jitters pro-*
*liferated into hysteria.*

*He wasn't the only one who had issues, however, because as he*
*was kissing Amy, Liz was kissing Steve, her old high school sweet-*
*heart. Nothing was making sense to either of them and they both*
*contemplated calling the wedding off. Ben finally got to Liz only min-*
*utes before their wedding was supposed to start. As they looked into*
*each other's eyes, they fell deeply in love all over again and it all be-*
*came clear. They immediately called off the wedding and took their*
*honeymoon to Hawaii, where they got married under a waterfall.*
*The moral of the story is: love is not easy but it is simple.*

I WASN'T SURE IF I EVEN NEEDED TO WRITE THIS CHAPTER, but in today's
age of rampant divorce an 1, more importantly, lack of realized love,
I decided that it was quite important. I've read in several places that
love is a "verb" or action, as opposed to a common thing. This is
most certainly true, and you need to live it in that manner or you will
be terribly unsuccessful as a person. Enough said, you'd think, but
unfortunately in this modern world, none of us get this very simple
concept.

One of the most important things about love is that it is a promise, and that's why we have vows. I'm not sure about you, but I've made many promises in my life. Some I've kept, others I've broken. You can probably relate. As a statement of how important your love is, it's a nice touch to talk about and write the vows yourselves. We happened to use very traditional vows because we believe in that stuff. We also made a few minor changes that made the vows more personal, and that worked out well. Here they are:

> *I take you (insert name) to be my wife/husband from this day*
> *forward,*
> *To join with you and to share all that is to come,*
> *To give and to receive,*
> *To speak and to listen,*
> *To inspire and to respond,*
> *And in all our life together,*
> *Be faithful to you,*
> *Until death parts us.*

When you break it down, most people don't really follow the vows that they take anyway. Maybe that's because they use the traditional ones that don't mean anything to them. From my perspective, everyone should write their own and if they don't believe "till death do us part," they should just say, "till something better comes along." Yes, that's pretty cynical, but it's also funny and quite common on Melrose Place.

I know this is a scary topic for men because we aren't in touch with strong emotions like love except when it comes to inanimate objects like golf clubs. However, we need to get past this problem when it comes to marriage and here are some quick and easy suggestions that you can easily follow. First, there's the old problem of not knowing if you're in love at all and trying to figure out what it should feel like when you are. That's a tough one that I don't even want to touch but I'm totally fearless, so I will anyway. Love is the most complex emotion in the human experience. It's even more intense than hate, greed, or revenge because it involves going against all your animal instincts of selfishness and putting the needs of another ahead of yourself.

One quick example: My wife misses me when I'm out of town. That's not love. However, the fact that she would rather experience the feelings of loneliness while I'm away than ask me to sacrifice a weekend trip with the guys: that's love. She would rather that I be happy and have a good time with some friends without her than self-ishly want me to be with her constantly. It's as easy and hard as that.

So if you're getting married, I hope you've got that part totally figured out because you're not doing anyone any favors by faking it. Showing and acting on love is the next big step to take and women really need you to do that before and yes, even after the big day. Here are a couple of very simple but meaningful ways to show your feel-ings. Write a poem about the way it makes you feel when you look into her eyes or, even better, steal someone else's words to say what you mean. If it has to be a greeting card, that's fine or even writing out the words to one of your favorite songs, that's great too. Just make sure you mean it and make your promise of love a habit created together that you never break.

QUICK HINT: For all the men out there reading this book, the next two chapters may cause problems with women. With that said, they may also be a great way to learn and get a little luck, too. One idea would be to use Chapters 8 and 9 as discussion pieces before you get into big planning. Maybe both of you should read them and blame the negative sexist stuff on me. From there, you can come together and concentrate on working as a team. What a concept!

# 8

◆ ◆ ◆ ◆ ◆

## BEING A MAN

WOMEN ARE HOPELESSLY IRRATIONAL, BUT MEN ARE IDIOTS, so here's how to cope. Men of the world (of which I am one), get in the game! Since you're reading this, you must be either already involved or somewhat interested in getting involved in the wedding process. There is another possibility as well: Your significant other/fiancée/wife handed you this book and told you to read this chapter. If that's the case, welcome and get ready to have a clue for the first time when it comes to women.

Now, just so you know, I'm not a pretentious academic psychologist who has done hours of research and analysis of women. However, I am proud to be a sensitive guy and I get a lot of the things that most men don't, so if you're one of those, listen up. Women get major-league pressure from modern American society to have the perfect wedding. If you don't believe this, you're nuts. My wife was a jock, tomboy, low-maintenance woman, and even *she* knew what kind of diamond she wanted and bought tons of wedding magazines.

Anyway, when women get stressed, which in general is more often than men in today's society, they need someone to empathize and care. This is where you step in. Women will get tons of pressure to pick out the perfect plates, flowers, songs, dress, ring, hair, shoes, and more. You are obviously an idiot and know nothing about any of these things, so you're at a terrible disadvantage. However, you need to learn a little and try to be helpful or you will remain single. Here's the first quick tip: Never respond to the question "What do you think?" with "I don't care." This answer proves you're an idiot and will result in a fight 99% of the time when it comes to wedding stuff. What you need to do is help your loving partner make the decisions she knows she can make herself. There are two ways to do this.

Either start learning about plates, flowers, songs, dresses, rings, hair, and shoes or take my advice. No one ever asked you to make the final decision, and if you want the truth, you won't be allowed to anyway. However, you need to give critical input. So, when you're in the moment of truth, try these three easy steps:

1. Put all other items out of your mind and concentrate carefully on the situation at hand;
2. Don't pretend to know stuff that you don't, but try really hard to weigh the options;
3. Give a thoughtful/supportive opinion and put it back in the expert's court to close.

Here are some more ideas for the idiotic gender. We need a lot of help to pull something like this off, which is understandable. We're also dumb as rocks about sentimental value so I thought I'd do some research and try to bridge the gap. An even better thought would be for you to come up with some ideas to make the big day special for the lady that you love. As an example, a gift for her on the wedding night is a great idea. No, you shouldn't get her something with leather or lace because that's actually a gift for you, moron. Get her something that she really likes that can have sentimental value for years. Your mind is drawing a blank, you say, so let me help you out. You could get a picture frame, a journal that you've started by capturing your feelings, a really nice card (check the back for Hallmark) with a note from you or the lyrics from your song, gift certificates for massages, manicures, or spas. Besides thinking of her needs, there are a few more problem areas that you as an idiot need to really watch out for:

- *China*: It's a waste of money! Seriously, no one uses china today and it will become even less useful in the new millennium. Now when I say china, I'm talking about the really expensive stuff that runs around $100 per plate and needs to be washed by hand. A couple quick points: first, why would anyone eat anything off a $100 piece of precious material? Secondly, how often could you possibly use something that nice? I can tell you right now, my wife and I eat most of our meals at the coffee table off our everyday plates, if not off a pizza box. We did end up getting two different types of place settings that were only around $50 per place setting. One is a pottery-type deal that has three different patterns in blue, green, and red made by Denby, which is pretty cool, if I say so myself. The other setting is a white base with a blue outline, which we intended for more formal use but we never even take it out of the cupboard. So, imagine how you'd feel if you had $1000 worth of plates sitting around that you never used.

- *Crystal*: It is an even bigger waste of money than china. My wife doesn't agree, but here's my thinking: The only thing worse than eating cheese macaroni off a $100 plate is drinking Busch Lite or wine from a box out of a $100 Waterford crystal glass. Simply asinine. So sway your lady towards the inexpensive glass-ware by using a line like "I'd hate to break one of those things" or "You know how klutzy our friends are, do we really want glasses like those?" This will work, I guarantee it. What you can do is help her pick out a couple of vases or candlestick holders in the really expensive crystal. However, be prepared to have to go back and buy the ones that no one gets you for the wedding. Even though they are expensive and you might think they suck, it's a slam-dunk for an anniversary/birthday/Christmas/Hanukah gift or something. Just keep the bridal registry sheets somewhere and go back to the store with them to make sure you get the right stuff. It doesn't get any easier than that.

- *Flowers*: I'm one of the lucky men who grew up on a farm and understand nature quite well. For most of us, however, we just have to punt and try to keep the budget in mind and get the ladies to make a decision and move on. Keep in mind that when you buy flowers out of season and just plain rare varieties, they will set you back a ton. Also, they die really fast as bouquets and end up getting thrown through the air and clawed at by single women, so don't overdo them. The only remnant after the wedding will be a few petals that probably get pressed in a journal somewhere.

- Shoes: Give up, you are screwed on this one. With men, we just want something that's comfortable, lasts long, and doesn't attract too much attention. With women, however, shoes are like fishing lures—you need a different one for every situation. Just step back and hope for leniency.

- *Hair, Nails, Make-up*: Here you are again in very deep trouble if you try to rationalize. After all, I showered, shaved, and applied my own gel on the big day. Women actually need to make a special trip to the salon weeks before the big day so professionals can practice for the wedding, and they charge you for that, too. For women, it is one of the only chances to be treated like a princess so just keep your distance and your mouth shut. If you ever see the bill, you will lose it but you'll never understand. It just becomes a good excuse to play a nicer golf course or drink more expensive beer to even the score.

# 9

♦ ♦ ♦ ♦ ♦

## FOR WOMEN

THIS IS THE SHORTEST CHAPTER IN MY BOOK because there's already tons of stuff out there for you and I'm no expert on women. Besides, you "get" the whole wedding deal. You just need some help to get your man involved. Remember, men are idiots, but women are hopelessly irrational, so get ready for some advice from a man on how to make it anyway. You may think I'm a pig, but really I'm not. I'm pretty thoughtful and a great husband but I'm also realistic and honest. I went after the guys in Chapter 8, so now it's your turn. I married a wonderful, sweet, caring, intelligent, low-maintenance woman who I love very dearly. However, I do believe that because of the unfair pressures by modern American society that push you as women to have the perfect wedding, you become terribly irrational during the wedding planning process. Since guys are idiots about plates, flowers, songs, dresses, rings, hair, and shoes (and you know that), you need to give them a break.

I'm not some hopeless "Men are from Mars, Women are from Venus" believer but there are some things you need to do to get what you need from your man and still get to the right decision for the wedding, too. During the planning process, there will be a time when you're at a crossroads between the classic design from Wedgwood and the contemporary pattern from Dansk. You will start getting worried that you're going to make the wrong decision and you'll look to your man for support and immediate assistance with this decision. Are you nuts? There's very little chance that he can help you out. He's an idiot, remember? However, you will be tempted, in your irrational stress, to lob a question like "What do you think?" out there. The answer may unfortunately end up being "I don't care," which will end up in a fight 99% of the time. However, I'm giving you the opportunity to stop that scene before it starts by giving you three easy steps to follow:

1. Narrow down the choices and clearly lay out your specific question;
2. Honestly give your opinion and ask for support and validation in this decision;
3. Be thankful and supportive of his response, make the decision and move on.

If you are really thoughtful, try to find a key role for your man and trust him to fulfill it: budgeting, acting as a human shield for you, delegating, or managing the lists, just to name a few. After all, you do love him and should know him pretty well, so don't expect too much or set him up for failure.

# 10

• • • • •

## THE BRIDAL REGISTRY

*Rob loved Jenny and they had been engaged for six months already. He had survived many wedding-related ordeals and thought he was home free. Not even close, Bud. The two most dreaded words to an almost-married guy are not "I'm pregnant" but "bridal registry." (Cue the scary organ music.) Jenny liked nice things and he liked that about her but he had no idea what he was in for.*

*Even after having several arguments and sacrificing decent golf time on Saturdays, Rob had nothing to show for his work but a long list of gifts that he would never understand or use. He had no idea what anyone would ever do with Waterford Crystal wine goblets at $67 each. All he could think about was how much the wine was going to cost. Next came the collectible china with painted flower patterns for a little more than $100 per place setting. Did they really need 10 sets of this stuff? They didn't even know 10 people that he would trust with those plates. After all, $1000 would buy a real swell set of golf clubs, half a hot tub, or satellite television for a year. Moral of the story: it's not for you, it's for her. Just try to find a comfortable chair and remember that you don't have to pay for any of this stuff.*

THE BRIDAL REGISTRY IS THE BIGGEST MAN-KILLER IN HISTORY. It's also a great way to get the stuff your fiancée really wants. One huge problem is that tons of people don't go by the list anyway because they either think they are creative or they are just plain dumb. Try not to get too stressed about it; just get ready to consume Excedrin by the handfuls and return a lot of towels. Here's how to get through the whole deal and come out alive.

I'm sure you'll get to register at the most boring of all department stores for towels and spatulas and all that. I would also recommend that you pick a fun store to register at that includes stuff you care about. Ours happened to be Crate & Barrel, but Target and REI are cool choices, too. One couple we know had a ton of camping stuff on their registry. They asked for a tent and stove and new sleeping bags, too. Remember that this is the only time in your adult life (no more Santa) that you get to make a huge list of all the things you want so live it up. As a man, you need to get involved to keep yourself interested and entertained. Here are some things that may be fun for you to register for:

- That new pair of jeans you'll need for all the weight you'll gain. Be prepared to get the veto from fiancée and store representatives alike;

- Anything to do with the garage or back yard, like a new gas grill, a lawn mower, or tools of any kind;

- Some things for the home like cutlery (that's knives for the cheap seats), or any glassware that will hold men's alcohol like beer mugs and highball glasses;

- Finally, pay attention when you start picking out the stuff for your bathroom, if you have one. Make sure you get some dark towels with no patterns. That and a toilet are all you need.

Now that you've got the stuff you need, here are a few quick suggestions to keep you from popping a bolt during the registration process like I did. First, make an appointment with the usually snotty bridal registry people. If you just show up, they will be out drinking a latte and will have no time for you. Plus, they will think you're unorganized and boorish and will probably not help you, even if you ask politely. For best results, set the appointment during a slow time at the store or you may have to wait in line to pick out a toilet rug. You may want to get this whole ordeal started about six months before the big day and definitely before any big holidays or your birthdays. This way, the people who really love you will be able to buy you stuff you really want *before* your wedding, too.

The next thing that will make your life much easier is bypassing some of the smaller and more boring things and buying them yourself. Don't spend your hard-earned time fighting over which features you need on a toaster. Just pick cool stuff that costs at least $10 per piece or comes in sets that cost over $10.

Also, since most bridal registry assistants are far from helpful, I made note of some other important stuff to remember. It is a great idea to have the gifts sent to your parents' home if you have that luxury. Let them coordinate the gifts and stack them in their basement or in your old room or something. Especially if you're not shacking up and are moving into a new home right before the wedding, all you need are more boxes to organize. You can have the address designated on your registry and that works out very well. You can also have cards sent to you when something is purchased that's on backorder from the warehouse. You may not care, but it's actually helpful to know. Also, make sure you are insistent in asking for discontinuation information on your patterns and items that you pick out. If you register a whole season in advance and find out two weeks before your big day that your dishes have been discontinued, you will have tons of back-orders and other problems.

As you may have guessed, I hated this process but it probably won't be as bad for you. However, it does have the potential to be much worse. Do your best to work together but readily admit that you're at a disadvantage and try to keep on a schedule so you don't waste a whole weekend. One huge secret that the idiots who are supposed to be helping you may not share is that you can pick up a checklist ahead of time and browse on your own before you come in for your appointment. They don't want you to know this because the more time they waste, the more job security they have. This is a key step in the process and you need to fight through the block because then you can get your actual picks done in less time. It's just like researching the best players for fantasy football before draft day instead of going in cold. I honestly hope you have more fun than I did, as my experience wasn't healthy.

*Section II: Details*

# 11

♦ ♦ ♦ ♦ ♦

## SITE SELECTION

As I said in the introduction, the easiest thing to do is fly to Vegas and get hitched in one of the many fine chapels by a middle-aged man dressed like Elvis. However, if you're set on a more traditional ceremony, this chapter will help you out.

There are a lot of options out there for sites. My wife and I went with a church, and many people like the added spiritual dimension and formal setting that a church offers. With churches however, there may be plenty of red tape. Some churches will charge you just as much as a country club if you're not a member. Even at a church where you are a member, good luck getting prime time like June, July, and August. Also, don't expect the church to organize anything for you. You will probably have to pay them for the organist, janitor, and maybe even the pastor. Which I guess is only fair, but be prepared for the little nickel-and-dime charges. After all, God has never been free.

Churches are beautiful and formal and perfect for most weddings but there are also some limitations. Most pastors and churches will limit your use of music and provide lists of appropriate material for readings as well. This is their prerogative. They work for God and will make censorship decisions at will. You're also subject to their preset schedule as well. For example, if you have some kind of holiday wedding planned, the church may already be booked. We were married the Saturday before Palm Sunday at Easter time and had to pick a less advantageous time, in addition to being pushed out in a hurry so they could set up for the service that evening. You can also forget about Christmas, or any other big church holiday that you may not even know about. I suggest checking with the church first. You should maybe even call immediately after you get engaged. If you're in some incredibly romantic place like atop a mountain, use your cellular phone.

You should by all means not be limited to churches for your ceremony. I've seen many beautiful weddings in city or national parks and many weddings in soap operas take place in back yards or on boats. Go for it. Remember that this is your special day and you should make it a reflection of your personality. My cousins were married in Montana at a yacht club and followed their ceremony with a regatta. My best friend from elementary school was married in Yellowstone National Park by a Forest Ranger and used a couple mountain men as witnesses. We even saw a couple get married on our honeymoon on the beach in Jamaica. Go ahead and think out of the box. It will hopefully only happen for you one time so make it great.

As far as the reception goes, you have many more choices and it can be difficult to come up with one that works. It was for us. We did the hotel and country club circuit trying to find the right ambiance and convenience for our guests. This was not easy. We could have gone with really cheap or really expensive, and contrary to popular belief, cost was not necessarily indicative of service and class.

Here are a few quick hints on making the decision easier. Make sure you meet face-to-face with the Manager or Coordinator or whatever they are calling themselves these days. You and many of your other vendors will need to spend time with this person and you need to feel very comfortable that they are not only competent but also congenial. Don't be fooled; just because someone is in the "service" industry does not mean they have any kind of clue on how to treat people. Besides the people factor, make sure you taste the food. Any facility worth its weight in garlic mashed potatoes will gladly let you taste entrées and salads and everything to be sure you get what you want.

Ask the facility to help you organize and secure the gifts that people bring for you as well because it's a very important and often overlooked detail that you won't have the time or energy to take care of. Also, confirm the flexibility to use outside vendors for food, decorations, entertainment, and similar services. Some places will restrict these freedoms; for example, they may not allow you to bring in your own alcohol or food. You may think that this sounds fair until you hear that the charge for a keg of beer is $175 instead of $50 from your local liquor store.

As an example, we picked a Radisson Hotel in a suburban location near our home. It turned out beautifully and was very convenient because our out of town guests stayed right there. It also ended up being in the middle of the price range, which was a surprise to us. They were very accommodating and helpful and they worked with our other vendors very well. The flower, cake, and DJ people found them to be very cooperative and for this, we were quite thankful. We also ended up having the rehearsal dinner at the restaurant in the hotel. We had looked around at several other places but were not able to find a restaurant that met our needs. The hotel staff bent over backwards and did exactly what we needed. Enough unsolicited plugs for Radisson International, you say. I agree, but they do deserve it from my perspective.

# 12

* * * * *

## THE CAKE—
## EVERYTHING IN MODERATION,
## INCLUDING MODERATION

THE CAKE IS A VERY BIG DEAL when it comes to weddings. You have no idea how big a deal the cake is until you see the prices! "Sticker shock" pretty much sums it up. You may be asked to pay hundreds of dollars for a cake. Yes, it's still made with flower and eggs and stuff, but it's purely an issue of packaging. The designs in the frosting, the pillars to hold the layers up, or the plastic bride and groom must be really expensive. If you believe that, you'll also believe that some facilities will actually charge you $1 per slice to cut the damn thing, too. It's insanity.

If you want the truth, no one even sees the cake unless you're planning on having your new bride jump out of it. The cake usually ends up off in a corner somewhere and you take a few pictures with it and then after dinner, you eat it. That's clearly not worth $1000! Especially if you do a honeymoon in a warm place, you won't even eat the cake because you need to look slim on the beach. Just have the people who are doing your dinner throw in your favorite dessert for free, you'll enjoy it more and no one else will notice. We had some friends who had their wedding catered by LeeAnn Chin's Chinese Cuisine and they served excellent carrot cake and fortune cookies for dessert. Problem solved.

So far, you're thinking, "Skip the cake." Bad idea, and one that I would not support. Life is difficult, and everyone deserves cake. As the chapter heading says, "Everything in moderation, including moderation." You need to eat cake, just don't spend $500+ on it. There are a few ways to get around the insane costs. First, if you want a fancy cake for decorative purposes, that's cool, but just get a really small one that will feed the wedding party and close family alone.

You could even use it at the brunch or lunch you have on the day after the ceremony.

Quick side note: don't ever freeze the top of your cake and try to eat it in a year. It will taste like refuse because for some reason that stuff doesn't keep for a whole year. You may as well take a picture of it and eat that on your anniversary. If you need nostalgia in your life, order a replica of your cake on your one-year anniversary, have a party and serve that. Sorry, back to the cake. For the bulk of the guests, as I said, they don't care what the cake looks like because they are going to eat it. I will borrow from Sprite, "Image is nothing, taste is everything." So order some really tasty but really simple sheet cakes of all different flavors and have a cake buffet: lemon, carrot, marble, chocolate-chip. Have your guests pick which one works for them, and then everyone is happy.

# 13

◆ ◆ ◆ ◆ ◆

## PHOTOGRAPHY/VIDEOGRAPHY—
## YOU'RE ON CAMERA

*Tracy and Mark hired a very desirable, award-winning photographer.
They were very anxious to see his interpretation of their love on film.
What they got did not meet their expectations. They sat for an engagement shot one evening and they knew they were in big trouble.
Jeff, as we will call him, had tons of background lights, four assistants, a fan, mirrors, and make-up. The set looked like a cross between the Sports Illustrated swimsuit shoot and Glamour Shots at
the mall. No good. Jeff burned through five rolls of film but couldn't
get one decent shot of Tracy and Mark. Moral of the story: keep it
simple, stupid.*

TAKE PICTURES AND VIDEOTAPE because you will forget things no matter how hard you try. Both my mom and mother-in-law take a picture
every 30 seconds of their waking lives. I used to think they were just
plain nuts, but then my mom told me that when she's old and de-
crepit, she wants us to leave her in a room with nothing but albums
full of pictures and she'll be happy. Your wedding, like your life, speeds
by on the wings of time and you miss a lot of it. That's kind of sad,
but whenever an event gets built up like this one does, there's too
much to take in. In order to preserve those memories somehow, I've
put together a few tips that have worked for others.

First, have a professional engagement sitting done. These are some
of the happiest professional pictures you will ever take. Trust me.
Our engagement shots turned out very well. Just think about it; that's
your last chance to take pictures with your fiancée before you're old
and married. You have to take that chance. Besides, that's the shot
that usually gets in the hometown newspaper for all your ex-girl-
friends and old classmates to see. You definitely want all those people

to see how happy you are without them, don't you?

For the wedding itself, you need a few things. I would suggest having a both professional photographer and an amateur one, as well as a videographer. Now I know you're reading this and saying to yourself, "What are we putting on here, a wedding or the Oscars?" That's a bit much, but it's a fair concern. Let me explain myself.

If we base the need for all this recording on the fact that you will not remember your own wedding without it, then we are all in a sane place. For starters, you really do need a professional photographer. Think about it for a second. Besides you and your spouse looking absolutely ravishing in clothes you will never wear again, think about your family and friends, too. At my wedding, my father, a 65-year-old farmer who likes ties and suits about as much as driving in the city, actually wore a tuxedo for the first time in his life. That was a thrill for all of us and I wouldn't have missed the chance to document that for anything. Even though it's expensive to go the professional route, they do a great job at getting group pictures of family and friends and will take a bunch of shots of the happy couple as well. This also took a lot of burden off our moms' shoulders because otherwise they never end up in any pictures, and they looked pretty good, too.

A few tips about getting the right photographer. Get referrals from other people and make sure you're comfortable with the person doing the pictures. I was in one wedding that drove me crazy because the photographer was the most annoying person ever. It was a small town in Minnesota, and she may have been the only one around, but come on. She was probably great with children because she had that ridiculous little voice and said things that rhymed trying to get everyone to smile. No good. Also, you could end up with someone who has the camera in everyone's face the whole time or follows you up the aisle and into the bathroom. That is a nightmare as well.

Specify what you want very clearly and make sure they understand. Also, to prevent a really big catastrophe, ask if they have film in the camera. You might laugh, but seriously, it happened to someone I know and needless to say, it was terrible. If you ever happen to need a photographer in the Minneapolis area, Linda's Photography in Delano, Minnesota is the best on service and follow-up, hands down. In fact, if you're willing to pick up airfare, Linda and her crew might even fly across the country, too. The key is to find experienced people who care about your wedding and listen to the things that are important to you.

Next, let's talk amateur photography. Even though the pros are quite good and they get all the really important shots, they do a lot of posing. Now posed shots are good, but they don't capture all of the personality behind the people and unless you want to pay big bucks, the pros won't be around for the whole night either. I know that a lot of people buy those disposable cameras and put the responsibility on their guests, but I don't like that idea. Let me tell you why. First, don't trust your guests. I've seen some people come up with no photos at all because those seated at the tables were too scared to use the cameras. I've also seen a number of pornographic photos on those cameras from people who were a little too comfortable in front of a lens.

If impromptu shots are what you're looking for, this is the best plan: Hire a close friend who's not in the wedding to go around with your camera and shoot all day and night. One really good idea that worked well for us was asking the significant other of one of our ushers. That worked out great because her guy was busy the whole time and she was more than willing to help us out. We got tons of great pictures and were very happy.

Last but not least, we have the video. When we first thought about it, we were a little freaked out, the same way we are freaked about filming the birth of our children. You know, it's a personal moment and you don't want a camera in your face. It's kind of like being a movie star getting chased by the paparazzi, if you know what I mean. Hopefully you don't, but that's beside the point. There are some videographers who work harder and take their job more seriously than "Dateline NBC." They will also charge you well over $1,000 for their craftsmanship. These ridiculous idiots will drive you crazy and will over-produce your wedding. If you want that, hire James Cameron and get someone else to play you.

If all you want is a video so you can watch the ceremony years later, which we think is great, here's the deal. I'm sure you have friends with expensive video equipment. If not, rent some. All you really need are a couple of cameras and tripods. We had one of our ushers, who is a gadget king, set up one camera at the back of the church and one (unobtrusively) at the front of the church as well. He just hit "record" about 15 minutes before the ceremony started and "stop" after it was over. What we ended up with was some really good footage of our big day. You could also ask a friend to set up the same process at the reception too, but we didn't go that far.

If you do choose to go the professional route, clarify your wants with the artist for both the filming itself and the editing, too. I've seen perfectly good footage ruined by a bunch of cheap special effects and cheesy music. Whatever you do, keep it tasteful and timeless. This may not get you an Oscar for cinematography but it will make you happy and preserve your memories.

# 14

♦ ♦ ♦ ♦ ♦

## PAPER

Yes, you do need to kill a few trees in order to pull off the perfect wedding. Although I have seen an 800 number and e-mail address for RSVP purposes, the good old US Mail is still the delivery channel of choice for invitations and thank-you notes. It's also rather difficult to do a cyber-program for the ceremony itself and using an overhead projector for the program might be a little tacky. So we're left with good old-fashioned paper, which is unfortunate because all the tree huggers are putting pressure on the logging industry, which in turn is curbing production and driving the price of paper upward. Sorry for the political interlude but it happens. Anyway, just because you're stuck with paper doesn't mean you have to get stuck with a huge bill. This is damn near the new millennium, for crying out loud, use a computer, design invites, thank-you notes, and programs yourself and run them off at Kinko's on some nice paper. They will even give you some tips, and fold them for you and everything, which is the greatest.

Production of invitations can be accomplished quite easily with a computer and word processing software package. It's been done and I've seen it. However, design and printing in color may be beyond most normal people's expertise. Also, as my wife put it at seeing homemade invites, "These look more like invites to a child's birthday party than a wedding." I had to agree with her. So, unless you've got some of Martha Stewart's blood in you and think you can pull it off, you may want to go with professional invites. This doesn't mean you need to spend thousands of dollars, however, because you can get it done reasonably. One great way to handle it is to go through either your photographer or tuxedo provider. If they are good businesspeople, they will give you a volume discount. We happened to go through our photographer and were able to pick the design out of some books and order at the same time we got our engagement picture taken. Do the math; that means one less trip to some lame store to pick them out.

Some quick tips on choosing the actual invites. There are a lot of pretty horrible designs and expensive extras that I would suggest avoiding at all costs. We picked a very plain but elegant design with navy blue ink, which was the color of our bridesmaids' dresses. That was actually my idea, if you can believe it. My suggestion on an extra to dump is the lined envelopes. Who cares if the envelopes are lined with the color of the ink? They are really heavy, which will push you into the next postal rate and they end up in the garbage anyway. Also, don't go with fancy folds and see-through layers either because again, they will just make you spend more on postage and don't add much value. Jump in here with all your manly practicality. She needs you and you can make a difference.

About eight weeks before the big day, you need to send the invitations. Don't mess with custom on this. People need time to plan and buy your gifts. Even if you did pick the prettiest ones, make sure that all the important information is included. And hopefully you've seen the episode of "Seinfeld" when George's fiancée dies from licking the cheap invites. Don't risk that; use a sponge to wet the envelopes.

Also, make the RSVP instructions quite clear. You will have a few stiffs who forget to send them back and you will also have people who misunderstand what you're asking them to fill in, so keep it simple. I have one friend who not only offered a stamped card as a return vehicle but also a toll-free voicemail box. It is truly the age of technology, huh? The next thing you know, everyone will get invites and RSVP over the Internet. Good grief. One other thing that you need to remember is to include info and directions on the reception site if it's different from the place you're actually getting hitched. One of our friends forgot that important info. Some people came late and missed the wedding but were planning on coming to the reception and missed that, too...because they had no clue where it was.

You also need to do invites to the rehearsal dinner for your wedding party and family and stuff. For these, I definitely recommend keeping it very simple, especially since you'll only need 25 or so. Getting a small number of professionally produced invites costs way too much and is overkill for something this simple. In fact, if you want to stick with tradition, the rehearsal dinner is also known as the groom's dinner and is usually funded and arranged by the groom's parents. So you can, with clear conscience, delegate the whole deal to them if you want.

One other thing: make sure you put a map and/or detailed directions to all important places in all your invitations. This is essential for people who are out of town or just plain clueless. You may also want to list telephone numbers for the church, hotels, and reception site for people who are disorganized and lose their map and directions. I know it seems ridiculous but there will be someone who gets lost and that will make you feel terrible, especially if they decide to return your really extravagant gift.

For our thank-you notes, we actually ordered the ones that matched the invites. Call us crazy if you want. They were relatively inexpensive and we liked the design and consistency so we went with them. The other key thing we were able to do was create a standard spiel for the inside of the note and imprint our names at the bottom as well. This is a great way to limit the writing you have to do on each card by allowing you to write only a quick and specific note instead of the standard "Thanks so much for being a part of our special day, blah, blah, blah." This is another place where I would support inexpensive alternatives like running off a standard letter from a computer or buying a pack of 100 blank thank-you notes from a paper warehouse type of place. Thank-you notes are another tradition that no one really cares about unless they don't get one, so don't waste a lot of time on them.

You also need programs for the ceremony because modern Americans have a very short attention span, and we really like to know what's going on at all times. So, you should probably do a program of some sort for the ceremony. Besides keeping everyone filled in, it's a great place to list your family and attendants and also do some thank-you's. Be sure to include the order of ceremony and also any songs you may want everyone to sing together. This is helpful because not everyone will be familiar with the ceremony or songbooks that may be available at your site. If I were you, I wouldn't buy professional programs from the invitation people. They're expensive and end up on the floor of the church or being colored on by children during the boring parts.

One useful item to include either on the program, as an insert in the thank-you note, or as a sticker, is your new address so people will have that in print. This is a nice feature since the invites usually come from the bride's parents' home, and no one will have your new address unless you've been shacking up for several years prior to making it official. (No judging from me as made clear by Chapter 6.)

# 15

◆ ◆ ◆ ◆ ◆

## THE WEDDING GOWN

*Matt was a simple farm kid. He was in way over his head. It was a sunny Saturday afternoon several months before the wedding (it's always sunny when stuff like this comes up). Sara's mom and best friend came to town to take her shopping. There was only partial disclosure about the shopping deal and Matt didn't get out in time. He innocently got into the driver's seat and they headed downtown. After all, they promised to buy him lunch if he drove. What he didn't know was going to come back to haunt him: This was wedding gown shopping!*

*Not only did this mean there was no way he was getting lunch at a decent time but he wasn't even going to get a decent place to sit and wait. After all, wedding gown shops have no time or place for men. Not only was he prevented from seeing Sara and her dress but because of the other women prancing around in their underwear, he actually had to sit outside and wait. It wasn't that cold out on the street and he wasn't that hungry but he was that much closer to understanding that what you don't know can hurt you. Moral of the story: run when you hear the word "gown."*

GENTLEMEN, DO YOUR BEST TO STEP OUT OF THE LOOP AT THIS POINT. Custom and superstition say you're not supposed to see the dress before the wedding day and common sense and I will tell you that you don't want to ever see the bill. These gowns get obscenely more expensive every day and the more simple they are, the more you will have to give up eating to pay them off. Hopefully, your bride has some friends or family nearby to help her pick the dress out. Even if that's not the case, you don't want to get involved anyway. Guys will never understand the mystique of the gown. For guys, they are poofy and white and you can't run in them and, most importantly, they usually have like a hundred thousand buttons to undo on the wedding night, which tire you out completely before you even get nude.

You need to set a general budget amount and make sure that your bride sticks to that because she will have the temptation to order the Vera Wang original that may cost more than a sport utility vehicle. There are several huge scams that you need to steer incredibly clear of with the "dress of a lifetime," as she will call it. How can it be the dress of a lifetime if you only wear it once when you're in your early twenties? That's a load of garbage. Anyway, don't let your starry-eyed fiancée or her goofy mom talk you into going dress shopping with them.

One more incredible scam after the wedding is the cleaning and hermetical sealing of the precious gown. They also have to put it in the largest box ever made and you almost have to build a special room to hold it. A dry cleaner will most certainly rip you off blindly to the tune of $200 to perform this important ritual. I have suits dry cleaned 50 times that have never cost that much. If you can't talk your wife out of it and convince her to put it in a plastic bag in the closet, just give up and take a bunch of money from her purse to buy booze and drown your sorrows.

# 16

♦ ♦ ♦ ♦ ♦

## MEN'S FASHION
## (OR LACK THEREOF)

WHILE MEN'S CLOTHING IS OBVIOUSLY MUCH LESS IMPORTANT than women's, a naked groom, groomsmen, and ushers will most certainly distract your guests. So what are you going to wear? You could go with the "Dumb and Dumber" look with baby blue and tangerine orange tuxedos with the ruffled shirts but naked would probably be better than that. My sister was married in the '70s and all the men wore brown tuxedos, which were hideous. Just as bad was my brother, who was married in the '80s and wore a white tuxedo. I, thank the gods, was married in the late '90s and had the smashingly good fortune of having few options but black. However, even if you don't have many options for screwing up your wardrobe, you end up looking bad with your regular clothes. Besides, you will be posing for several thousand pictures in your monkey suit so you better look good for the big day.

Here come the tips from a man who has picked out his own clothes since he was about eight. Yes, I've had my weak moments, like the time I dressed like Don Johnson (a la "Miami Vice") for my eighth grade graduation, but I've pulled it together since then so you can trust me. You may get some pressure to actually buy a tuxedo, but please stay away from the expensive department stores and do everything you can to avoid purchasing one. One member of the special couple is already buying a garment that will only be worn once. If that's going to happen, it may as well be for the woman alone. Besides, most men, including yours truly, gain several pounds in the first few years of marriage. This means that your svelte new tux won't fit after all the food you eat on the honeymoon. Don't get too depressed about the weight, though. For once in your life, you no longer need to impress the ladies. The woman you married loves you thin and a little chunkier, too.

I recommend renting for the entire wedding party and make sure you get the optional insurance policy, just in case someone pukes or rips a whole in the crotch while trying to do a dance that they aren't qualified to do. We happened to use Gingiss Formal Wear. There's one of them in every major mall, and they do a great job of helping you pick out what you need and they also usually give the groom his tux for free because they fleece the rest of the wedding party for full price. Ha ha. The only way to go for the groom is black. I have seen a few grooms actually go with the black pants and white dinner jacket, but you risk being asked for drinks all night if you try to pull that off. Your other problem is looking like an employee on "Fantasy Island." Both problems can be easily avoided by going with black. Don't ask me why black is the color for weddings and funerals. Just do it.

There are several styles for tuxedos, almost as many as wedding gowns. For the groom, most men go with tails to differentiate themselves from the stiffs who actually had to pay for their rentals. I, for one, don't really like tails that much unless you're playing the violin at Orchestra Hall. Besides being uncomfortable to sit in, I think they look dumb, but don't believe me. After all, what do I know? You need to try on several different options and see what ends up being most comfortable for you. I would advise bringing a lady with you, preferably the bride if you are planning to see each other's outfits before the wedding day, but the maid of honor, your sister, or another female friend is great, too. If you're going to do that, however, bring one of the guys from your wedding party as well to balance out the female perspective. That way you won't end up with a look that fits more on the Broadway stage than on your body. Face it, you may need some help to pick out the best look and if you're going with multiple sets of eyes, make sure they are objective or they at least balance each other out.

Some other options you need to consider are single-breasted, double-breasted, or three-button. That's why you need to try a few options on so you can figure out what looks best. As far as other basic accessories go, you do need pants, but they are quite plain and

I wouldn't worry about them too much. Again, just go with black.

The real problems come in with the other pieces of the formal ensemble. You need to pick out a shirt, and I recommend a white or off-white number, depending on the color of your bride's gown. Believe it or not, there are as many shades of white for wedding gowns as there are for interior house paint. Picking either should be strictly avoided. The shirt is not too tough; just please, no ruffles. It does get pretty sticky when it comes to the rest of the outfit, however.

There are a lot of different styles of ties, and you can go in many different directions. We decided to go with the plain color shirt with button covers instead of ties. This made all the men happy, including my dad who hates ties more than he hates sitting still. Another piece of the puzzle is: cummerbund or vest or nothing? For us, the vest worked out very well, but those aren't easy to choose either since there are several styles, colors, and textures. From my perspective, you have to go with a vest rather than cummerbund, unless you're getting married at a prom and you are 17. As far as style and color goes, please, I beg you, go with something very simple and muted. You're not trying to be a peacock. You're trying to look formal and classic. Don't match any accessories with the bridesmaids' dresses. This tends to cheapen the entire deal and makes everything look a bit too contrived and also dopey. Again, there will be many pictures and you want them to be timeless, so dial it back a notch and keep it simple.

Finally, it comes down to shoes. These things suck. Who is the complete idiot who invented these ridiculous excuses for shoes? They don't even have regular laces and tongues, for heaven's sake. The creator of these things must have been the same idiot who came up with the idea to make women walk around in high heels. Stupid! Make sure you tell the guys to bring something more comfortable to wear around between pictures and at the reception, too. Sneakers like Converse Chuck Taylors are pretty popular, but everyone should have some more comfortable dress shoes.

I have known a few grooms and wedding parties alike who have gone with suits instead of tuxedos. This is a great option, and I would support that 100%. You can still try to coordinate stuff like ties, which will make you look organized and classy. However, this also leaves the door open for one of your moron ushers to show up with a hideous sport coat from the 1979 Arnold Palmer collection at Sears and ruin the whole deal. You know the friends that I'm talking about. You were one step away from them without your mom or the woman you're marrying.

# 17

◆ ◆ ◆ ◆ ◆

## THE HONEYMOON

*Brad and Diane booked the honeymoon of a lifetime. Unfortunately for them, it would feel like a lifetime. They were very excited about their seven-day Hawaiian cruise but also a little nervous (not about that). They both suffered from motion sickness. In fact, neither of them could ride roller coasters or even watch them, for that matter. So, they did the prudent thing and sought medical advice. When faced with this issue, their physician did what all good ones do: She wrote them a prescription. They were satisfied and after the wedding were on their way to paradise. Both Brad and Diane were good little patients and took their medicine at the airport before getting on the plane. They had no idea what was coming.*

*The next thing they knew, they were in Hawaii boarding the biggest ship they had ever seen. Neither of them was feeling very well, but they thought it was just nerves. They were escorted to their room and found it to be quite nice, which was a good thing because they didn't leave it much for the next seven days (no, not because of that). They had an allergic reaction to their prescription which made them run high fevers and break out in hives. If that wasn't enough to deal with, there was a little vomiting mixed in because they had to deal with the motion sickness without medication. At least they were together in the closet-sized bathroom. Moral of the story: get a second opinion when it comes to medical care.*

I'LL KEEP THIS ONE SHORT AND SWEET—you need to take some time off right after the wedding because you deserve it. Figure out a way to take a week, even if you have to go camping together in a local park. Extravagance is not the key component here, but time together to celebrate your newly committed love is. We took a seven-day Caribbean cruise that was fantastic: no hives and no vomiting. I would have to say that a cruise is the number one honeymoon activity (other than the obvious) because you don't have to worry about anything except which SPF sunscreen to use and which buffet to choose. These ships are absolutely amazing, if you ask me.

We sailed out of Miami to Haiti, Jamaica, Grand Cayman, and Mexico. We sunbathed, snorkeled, hiked, and sailed like the rich and famous. Out boat was equipped with seven bars, a health club, two swimming pools, five dining rooms, and 75 other honeymoon couples who didn't see much more than their rooms. Actually, the only potential problems are seasickness and getting kidnapped or robbed in Jamaica. For Jamaica, just stay on the ship. Seriously, the Jamaica I saw was beautiful but also crawling with unapproved taxi drivers, crooked merchants, and constant offers to buy drugs. Unless you're into that, you should pass.

For seasickness, make sure you ask a pharmacist and take some Dramamine or something. Don't overreact to this potential problem, but if you have a weak stomach be careful with a cruise. The other person who will be able to help you out with this problem is your travel professional. They can usually tell you what the water will be like where you are going and that most large cruise ships are really quite stable. If you have doubts, don't risk it on your honeymoon. Stay on land. If the water is where you need to be, at least avoid hurricane and iceberg season or take a short cruise for three days that's part of a longer vacation.

Cruises are expensive and they nickel-and-dime you like crazy on those boats. They even take your picture several hundred times a day and rip you off by selling it back to you for thousands of dollars. Don't even try to get out of buying them, both because they look great and you may never get on a cruise again. The other major expenditure is alcohol. First, you will get real thirsty real fast in the hot Caribbean sun and there will always be someone there to sell you a beverage. Second, the "Paradise Punch" in the commemorative glass will run you like $9 and everything gets charged back to the room so you don't realize how many of them you put away. Scary.

We have several friends who took equally fun and relaxing trips that never broke the bank. We know people who drove into Wisconsin and stayed at a different bed and breakfast every night of the trip. This won't work as well if you live on either coast but if you do, stay home. You're already near the ocean. We also know people who went to Mackinac Island for a week but only stayed in the expensive places three out of seven nights and the Super 8 for the rest of the time. You can certainly pull off a great trip on a long weekend if you have a combination of little vacation from work and even less money. Talk with your friendly neighborhood travel professional or just use the Internet. It's pretty easy to come up with something inexpensive in today's travel market.

One caution: if a trip is really cheap and sounds too good to be true, it probably is. Don't get ripped off by some resort somewhere that no one has ever heard of. Keep the trip simple and reputable for safety. Finally, make sure you confirm your reservations. If you don't, you might end up like some friends of ours: 2:00 a.m. in a small town in Minnesota with the groom in his tux, bride in her gown, and no room in the Inn. Not good. I'm sure you can come up with something that's in your budget and also fun and relaxing. Just make sure you do it.

# 18

◆ ◆ ◆ ◆ ◆

## SHOWERS

*Craig and Beth had lots of cool friends. It just so happens that none of them were involved in planning their couple's shower. This is bad. Not only did they not get input on the guest list but they were also in the dark about the theme: "Fun things that Craig and Beth can do together." People with a sense of humor could do a lot with that but these people were born in a place where nothing was funny. The whole deal was doomed from the beginning because there was too much planning and not enough time to just hang out and drink. Every lame party game was orchestrated throughout the evening. They began with that game where everyone has a name on their back that they have to guess but they can only ask like three questions. It was further complicated by making it a couples event and calling it, "Guess the Famous Lovers." Craig and Beth actually had their own names on their backs. Blech! The nausea increased all evening before the party cleared out after a rousing game of "Wedding Pictionary." Moral of the story: you can't plan fun.*

SECOND ONLY TO THE BRIDAL REGISTRY IN BEING PAINFUL FOR MEN EVERYWHERE IS THE SHOWER.

The typical "girls only" shower isn't terribly frightening. After all, you get the exemption and get to go out and play golf or sit home and watch the game on TV. Right? This may be the case for showers put on by old and boring relatives like an aunt or your church or something. However, beware of the so-called "personal shower," which may be little more than a thin cover for the bachelorette party. The personal shower may be good for you in some ways because your wife will more than likely get some very attractive lingerie from her friends and you shouldn't thwart that. However, for the shower that turns into a gaggle of women dragging your wife into singles bars for the last time wearing a veil, beware.

For every low class friend that you have, your fiancée has a perfect match. Not that you need to get overly protective or anything but it certainly makes sense to agree to some guidelines for the last great singles party before strapping on the ball and chain for good. Even worse than having your wife paraded around bars with condoms stuck all over, life-savers taped to a shirt that says "a buck a suck," or instructions to get other men's underwear is the dreaded "couple's shower."

Couples' showers suck, no matter how you cut it. Don't let anyone talk you into believing the contrary. They might even tell you that it will be really fun and you will get cool gifts like tools. Unless the hosts split you up at the door and send all the men out to the garage, where there is a big screen TV and beer, it's a lie. To get the gifts, you usually have to dress like an idiot and play ridiculous games invented by people who are too boring to have impromptu fun. Not even my wife, who is a woman, by the way, likes those stupid shower games.

Seriously, if someone offers to do a couple's shower, get some veto authority and ask to get involved with the guest list, too. All you really need to do is find some cool hosts, buy some beer, and invite fun people. You should not allow the planning of more than one "event" for the whole evening and should have very few rules at all. I've seen some pretty cool ideas. I went to one shower where everyone brought hats for the bride and groom. That allowed for some creativity and also gave everyone a chance to publicly tease the couple of honor. We ended up with a pair of hats that has been passed around. It became a tradition for each new couple to autograph them and pass them on to the next lucky couple. Also, you can send out a rule for gifts for the couple, like telling people to bring something that's not on the bridal registry that the couple will absolutely need after they are married. Give them a price limit, too, like $10 or less. That will keep it simple for sure. If you don't take some action, you may end up wasting a perfectly good Saturday afternoon with a bunch of idiots playing "Wedding Pictionary." Cripe!

# 19

♦ ♦ ♦ ♦ ♦

## THE BACHELOR PARTY

*Mike and his buddies were all jocks, so they had to exemplify this at the bachelor party. Thankfully, no strippers or drugs were involved but that didn't keep them from nearly ruining the wedding. One of Mike's friends had connections and he got them into the college arena to play some hoops. It was agreed upon that, for Mike's party, everyone would come over and play a game of pick-up basketball. It was a big testosterone thing and everyone was excited to live out their boyhood fantasy of playing big-time college basketball. On the night before the wedding, everyone showed up and got ready to rumble. The game was going well. Mike's parents and sister even dropped by to shoot some video of the event.*

*Then the unexpected struck. Mike, being a good athlete, decided to close out the evening with one last big dunk. He got his dad's attention so his skill would be captured on video and then he made his approach. Unfortunately, that would be his last attempt at a dunk. As he went up, something snapped and he came down with a thud. No one really knew what happened, but they knew it wasn't good because Mike was in a lot of pain and needed to go to the emergency room. After a long wait, they finally heard the news that he had ripped his patellar tendon and would be in a full leg brace for a few weeks.*

*The next call was the toughest. Mike spoke to Cindy (the fiancée) over the phone and told her the news. She cried, as was expected, but the show must go on. Mike wore the brace under his tuxedo pants and walked with a limp. He also endured the honeymoon in Hawaii with a serious leg brace and quite a bit of pain. The moral of the story is: take the night before the wedding off.*

No single event can cause more pain, headaches, and can-celled weddings than this one. The horror stories have become legends and have caused a lot of pain. If your friends are stupid enough to get out of hand, make it very clear to them that this is not the time or the place to do it. Here's a suggestion: Get everyone together and watch a football, baseball, or basketball game or rent some funny movies but avoid the following at all costs. Never let anyone get a stripper to come to your house and rub her body on you, unless its your fiancée. I know one couple who have been married for years, but their biggest hang-up is still the stripper who was a part of the bachelor party. In fact, the wife actually hates the guys who insti-gated it, even after all these years. That may be a bit much but still, was it really worth it? No way.

The old tradition of "one more big fling" is a thing of the past and a really stupid one as well. Never get really hammered on the night before your wedding, either. What could possibly be the point of getting totally drunk and whooping it up that close to the biggest day of your life? I know one guy who got so drunk on the night be-fore his wedding that he had to throw up right before he walked down the aisle. I know another guy who had obvious idiots for friends who put him on a bus headed for Montana after he passed out and never bothered to tell his fiancée. That wedding got called off. Thanks a lot, guys.

Not that you have to take advice from me but my bachelor party was the best one I've ever attended. We were married during "March Madness," the NCAA Men's Basketball Tournament (for non-sports fans). We were also very lucky to have our beloved Minnesota Golden Gophers in the "Great Eight" on the Thursday before our wedding. We all hung out at the hotel that my family was staying at and watched the game with some pizza, chips, and beer. It was the greatest and the Gophers even beat UCLA to advance to the dance! So my simple advice is to keep it clean and use your common sense. Please.

# 20

• • • • •

# THE LAST MINUTE

I USE THIS CLICHÉ AS A TITLE FOR THIS CHAPTER only because it sounded better than potpourri. This is a book for men after all. You shouldn't leave anything to the last minute because messing with fate is a big risk to take in the last hours before your wedding. Also, it is nice to enjoy the last minute instead of running around like a bride or groom with your head cut off. I'm just going to list a few things that need to be taken care of in the last several weeks.

One last minute item involves acquiring a marriage license. States vary on this but you're not actually married unless the referee and a couple of witnesses give you their autographs on that important piece of paper. I almost blew this detail. I went in about a week before the big day only to realize that, in the fine state of Minnesota, there is a five-day waiting period for getting married. Thanks to the NRA, you can go out and buy a shotgun on a moment's notice and shoot at people but you need to wait 120 hours to get married. This prevents people from making rash decisions about love - or maybe it just allows state employees to take their precious time creating the official document. Check early and take care of this item so your soon-to-be better half doesn't have to.

Gifts for the wedding party usually come late, too, and while these are a must, knocking yourself or the bank account out with them is not. In most situations, you are asking the friends and family involved in your wedding to rent tuxedos and buy impractical dresses that they will never wear again. This is fine, though. Don't feel guilty and try to make up for it with extravagant or perfect gifts. What goes around comes around and you'll more than likely be in their weddings, too.

My wife's idea was to buy the jewelry that her ladies would be wearing as the gifts. We spent about a thousand years trying to find the right earrings and bracelets. Not fun. I was having some trouble figuring out my gifts for the guys but jewelry was out for sure. I landed on some golf balls and my promise to hold a golf tournament as my treat to all of them. Unfortunately, our wedding was several years ago and I still haven't gotten the whole group together. I have managed to play golf with most of the guys and bought some beer for the rest of them.

One more quick thought for the last minute includes making sure you are packed and have your bags in a readily available place to take off for the honeymoon. Finally, make sure you go out and buy a newspaper from the big day so you can keep some of the headlines in your journal. Even if you're not sentimental at all, you may actually enjoy looking back and checking the front page, cartoons, and sports section from your wedding day in 70 or 80 years.

There is one other item that I feel obligated to mention only because my good friend Donald Trump told me to: pre-nuptial agreements. There has been much publicity surrounding the pre-nup and it's probably warranted. After all, let's say you're a billionaire or your fiancée is (either way, lucky you!) No, let's say that you're marrying someone with no money who's half your age and this is your third marriage. For those of you who fit this description, not only do you not need a pre-nup, what are you doing getting married anyway? Skip the wedding, give the money to charity, and just shack up instead. Now for the average Joe, which includes everyone I know, you usually don't have anything to divide up so what's the point? I don't know a single person who has a pre-nup. However, I do know some who have had nasty divorces before their 30th birthdays, so go figure.

I read somewhere that California, a very litigious state, was considering requiring pre-nuptial agreements to accompany all marriage licenses. Wow! The rationale behind it is that divorce proceedings clog up the court system too much. Tough break, why don't they just mandate that people must love each other instead? Or even better, how about requiring that divorce promises be added to the wedding vows like "I promise to be fair in divorce"? If you're really worried about it, talk to your lawyer. Otherwise, just hide a pile of money from your fiancée and start your life together by living a lie.

*Section III: The Big Daze*

# 21

♦ ♦ ♦ ♦ ♦

# THE REHEARSAL DINNER

*Todd was assuming that all the hard work and headaches were be-hind him on the eve of his wedding. That was hardly the case. It was really no one's fault, but the head table was only set with six places instead of eight. This was no problem for most families but it was a huge problem for Todd's divorced parents. If you do the math, six places left room for Todd and Sherry, Sherry's parents, and two more. Todd knew there was no way that his parents would sit next to each other without their dates and he knew there was going to be trouble.*

*An argument ensued and ended with Todd picking his dad and his new wife for the table and promising his mom a spot of honor the following day at the reception. Negotiating with their parents like they are toddlers is not something that most people expect to do at their wedding but it happened and it shook Todd up quite a bit. In fact, to make matters worse, Todd was so wound up that he forgot the name of his best friend's girlfriend of two years during introduc-tions. They broke up about a year later anyway, and that couldn't have been Todd's fault. Moral of the story: don't relax until you're safely on your honeymoon.*

IF YOU'RE GOING TO CUT CORNERS ON A WEDDING, the rehearsal din-ner is a pretty good place to do it. If you're having a rehearsal on the night before the wedding, you are obligated to feed the wedding party, especially if they busted their butts to get there from out of town. However, you don't need to serve them filet mignon. In fact, you could just do sandwiches or pizza at your parents' house if it works for you. The rehearsal dinner is a nice time to get together with your family and closest friends before the craziness of your wedding day, but keep it simple.

We actually ended up having dinner at the same hotel where our reception was held and that worked out great for everyone. Our out of town guests were already there and it happened to be close to the church as well. Dinner ended up being a pasta bar and a few of us who like meat (my wife is an herbivore) were able to order steaks as well. It was a small group and we had a separate little terrace all to ourselves, which was great for mingling. This event is a perfect time to give gifts to the wedding party and, if you're lucky, they might give you some funny stuff as well.

Our maid of honor and her husband passed on a gift of two hats that said "Honey" and "Mooner" respectively but my wife wouldn't let me wear the "Mooner" hat in public. You win some and you lose some. Also, my family put together a newlywed care package with some fun stuff like a classic love story movie, champagne, some snacks, sexy stuff for us to wear (lingerie and silk boxers), and whipping cream. It was tastefully done and fun, a great event for the night before the big day.

One last task that can be easily taken care of is clarifying the schedule for the following day and making sure that everyone has everything they need like tuxedos and shoes. We actually put together what I called a "script" for everyone to follow that included everything our people needed to know about the entire weekend. I sent this out to everyone ahead of time but also handed it out that night to make sure that it was clear to everyone. It seemed to help and got a few laughs, too. Here it is if you want to copy it:

WEDDING SCRIPT
*Friday*
6:30 PM Rehearsal at the church for the entire wedding party.
7:00 PM Rehearsal Dinner at the hotel, same one as the wedding reception.
*Saturday*
3:00 AM If you're up, think of me, because I'll be awake for sure, possibly drinking heavily but most likely watching Sports Center.

6:00 AM  Get up and do aerobics or something useful like getting your hair done.

12:00 PM  Be at the church for pictures, and be ready to smile. Bring your tuxes and dresses with you rather than wearing them so they don't get wrinkled. There are changing rooms at the church (boys and girls separated) that will be locked during the ceremony so no one steals your comfortable clothes. There will also be some food to snack on like bagels, fruit, crackers, and beverages.

2:30 PM  Pictures will be finished. Ushers start ushering, wedding party out of sight.

3:00 PM  Steve's hands will be sweating as he stands at the front of the church and watches everyone walk down the aisle in the following order:

> Michelle and Scott
>
> Carrie and Dave
>
> Polly and Peter
>
> Carrie and Kelly
>
> Justin and Cody (ring dudes)
>
> The Beautiful Bride–My hands will really be sweating now!

3:45 PM  We're hitched, and "Now We Dance!" (Actually we schmooze and eat first, but mark my words, we *will* dance.)

4:00 PM  More pictures at the hotel, followed by the receiving line.

5:30 PM  Pastor Dave leads the blessing, Jim gives a speech, and dinner is served.

7:00 PM  The first dance, or jig, or polka, or whatever you're into!

11:00 PM  The last dance! You don't have to go home, but you can't stay with us!

*Sunday*

7:00 AM  Anne and Steve leave for the Caribbean! Whoopee!

Now you might think that this is a bit much but then again, think of your friends: Some of them are morons. There are a couple of people in every group, especially in Generation X, who need clear instructions so they don't screw something up. This type of script is also good for the really anal people so they feel comfortable with all your expectations of them as well. They can even insert it right into their daily planners. Don't say this doesn't sound familiar. If nothing else, it will ensure that *you're* not late for anything important on the big day.

# 22

◆ ◆ ◆ ◆ ◆

## THE CEREMONY—
## SIMPLE YET MEANINGFUL

I HAVE TO BE HONEST WITH YOU: I wrote this chapter with a church in mind. However, I know people who chose to get married in a back yard, town hall, wedding chapel, or mall. The place is immaterial, but the components are very important. You can get it done in any setting except maybe in front of Lambeau Field on game day. Besides, do you really want that many toothless people at your wedding? Sorry, cheeseheads.

You can always tell a wedding where the couple puts time into planning the ceremony. It's actually, contrary to popular belief, the most important part of the entire day. This is where you actually say "I do," and all that. This is what people are coming to see, not the groomsmen dancing with their pants around their ankles. Actually, some people just came for the free dinner but what are you going to do?

Two things that really confuse people as they arrive at a wedding are the guest book and the gift situation. For the guest book, it may be nice to have an attendant of some kind but if you're like us and assume people can sign their name on their own, you can skip that. Also, it's really funny and sometimes annoying to watch people file in and stand in line for the guest book. It can be a bigger problem than you think because I've been at a few weddings that ended up starting quite late because people stood in line for the book instead of taking their seats. You should have one of the ushers or someone close the book about 10 minutes prior to kickoff so you can get people in their chairs on time.

Another common problem is caused by gifts. Many people lug their gifts to the ceremony, even though they know there is a reception following, because they are old or dumb. You should have someone standing around who can ask people to please bring the gift to the reception site instead. We went with two host couples who we relied upon to handle the autograph and gift questions, which worked out pretty well.

For the programs that you worked so diligently to design yourself, you also need some instructions. One good hint is to make sure that they both get to the site *and* get handed out. We went to a wedding once and were quite surprised at the absence of programs. We were even more surprised to get ours at the reception. They had been left in the box for the ceremony and were never handed out. This is another key job for the ushers or host couples.

When it comes to seating, please seat those who come first nearest the center aisle. If they arrive early, they deserve to get a good seat. The best way to pull this off is to rope off the center aisle and seat from the sides. This way, early birds get the best seats and no one needs to climb over others as they arrive. You may think that this is a really small thing and not worth worrying about, but people being seated is the first experience of the wedding, so you may as well make it positive.

Another big key to the ceremony is setting ambiance. Readings and music are great to have as part of your wedding, no matter what your beliefs are. They work well to set the appropriate tone and inspire thought. For us, we're boring Lutherans, and we went with a string quintet playing Vivaldi; a hymn by John Rutter; a soloist doing an original piece and the Lord's Prayer; and a reading from the Corinthians. If religion isn't your deal and you still want a reading of some sort, go with some poetry. No one has ever written more eloquently about love than William Shakespeare, with the exception of some modern punk rock bands. Just kidding. Pick some lines from Romeo and Juliet or Kate and Petruchio and read them to each other, or have someone with a good radio voice do some lines from Sonnet 116 (look it up, it's pretty great).

I was at one New Age wedding where they played Yanni and read some modern poetry that didn't even rhyme. I saw another where the bride's family broke into spontaneous song just like the Von Trapp's.

As far as music goes, anything goes or at least almost anything. I wanted to walk out of the church as husband and wife to Van Halen's "Can't Stop Loving You" from the "Balance" CD. That was vetoed by my more conservative mate, who thought it would make her 80+-year-old grandma cry.

Here are some examples of other music to avoid at weddings (a friend of mine actually sang these numbers):

- "Angel of the Morning" by Juice Newton. I think it's about a prostitute who just gets up and leaves every morning without expecting commitment. I don't even need to say why that's not entirely appropriate for a wedding.
- "A Whole New World" from Disney's "Aladdin," which is good for cartoons but probably not for people.
- "Glory of Love" by Peter Cetera. Fine for "The Karate Kid" but come on!
- My personal favorite, "Tears in Heaven" by Eric Clapton. It was "their song" but they obviously did too much acid.

Just do something musically and do your best to pick something moderately tasteful.

A message, sermon, or just a few kind words about the act of taking the plunge is also a nice touch. If you're going the church route, you may not have any control over what the clergy will say in the sermon. However, you may be able to suggest the passage from Scripture that they speak about. We went to one wedding where a Roman Catholic priest spoke for just under 30 minutes, and 25 minutes were about divorce. Needless to say, it dampened everyone's spirits just a bit. I don't remember the specifics of our pastor's homily but I remember that it was short and it made everyone laugh a couple of times and that is all I could have asked for.

Finally, when the crying is over and the wedding party has made their way out of the facility, it's a nice touch to have your ushers show guests out row by row. I've seen some brides and grooms personally usher everyone out themselves, which is touching, but frankly it takes too long. Especially if you're having a reception, just let everyone get out of there more quickly and get on with it. A lot of couples like to run through the crowd and hop into a limo to simulate stardom, and it's actually pretty fun. However, all the animal rights people have put an end to rice- throwing to protect the birds, so what are your options? I've seen several things from birdseed, which seems dumb, to confetti, which you may have to clean up, to bubbles, which are kind of cool. We actually kept it simple and clean and didn't give people anything to throw at all. Besides, we were married in March in Minnesota and people really didn't want to stand outside very long.

# 23

## THE RECEPTION—CELEBRATE
## AND DON'T FORGET TO DANCE!

*The wedding was beautiful and Jack and Lucy were at the head table
gazing into each other's eyes. Then it happened. Rick, Jack's best
friend, stood up to give the toast (or burn it, as you will see). It started
out innocently enough when Rick chronicled his long friendship with
Jack and Lucy but then he gave out way too much information. He
decided to close out the toast with a story of their trip out to Montana for another friend's wedding when Jack and Lucy first started
dating.*

*He told of Jack's incessant gas and diarrhea and how he just laid
in the back seat of the car and moaned. This was fine with Rick
because he got a chance to talk with Lucy. "The trip turned out just
fine," recounted Rick, "because later that weekend was the first time
that they did it. I think she felt sorry for him."*

*That wasn't even the end! He also dropped the bomb that the
two had lived together and let him stay with them when he came in
from out of town. Both of these tidbits were big hits with the Bible-
bangers from the small Minnesota town in which the wedding was
held. Mouths hung wide open, Lucy cried, and Rick finished up by
slamming his glass of champagne. Moral of the story: never let anyone from Montana do a toast at your wedding.*

HOPEFULLY, YOU TOOK MY ADVICE FROM CHAPTER 22 AND DECIDED
NOT TO HOLD YOUR GUESTS HOSTAGE IN THE CHURCH WHILE YOU USHER
THEM OUT YOURSELVES. If not, skip ahead a little and don't invite me
because I hate sitting in an uncomfortable church pew for 90 minutes
in 100 degree heat waiting for the bride to hug each person. Sorry,
bad memories. Bygones.

Anyway, you need some kind of receiving line for your guests at

◆ 104 ◆

the reception. The best situation is when you have some snacks and beverages for people to nibble on and no one line for people to have to stand in. A universal principle of America is that waiting in line sucks; therefore, make your line informal and possibly even optional. People with any kind of a clue or class know that it's polite to walk through a line and shake the hosts' hands. Our idea was to make ourselves the gateway to dinner and we formed a line about 45 minutes before the toasts were scheduled to take place.

As far as people go, those dopey traditions indicate that the line needs to include bride, groom, and parents. We were lucky to have all our parents with us and still married so we set it up like so: father of the bride, mother of the groom, me, bride, father of the groom, and mother of the bride. This way, someone who knows each of the guests who you are about to share an uncomfortable hug with will be standing next to someone who is unfamiliar. This ensures that you will have a name attached to the awkward sentiment from someone's 70-year-old aunt. One other problem is whether to hug or go with the firm handshake. From my perspective, the "wink and gun" gesture will do just fine but you usually need to touch people. When in doubt, shake one hand and do the back pat with the other.

Food is the big key and you may be thinking, what's the deal? Can't we just pick an entree and be done with it? I've said it before and I'll say it again: Nothing about weddings is ever simple. If you go with a hotel or country club for the reception, get ready for $30 per plate for the Chicken Kiev. Do the math on 250 people and get ready to max out the credit card. These aren't clients of yours that you need to impress, for crying out loud. Most of the guests are relatives you may not even know so serve them fish and chips in a basket. Just kidding. You can certainly have an elegant meal if that's what you want, but you also have several options. I know people who have done very nice buffets and saved money. I've also seen a barbecue wedding for 50 people as well. One of my favorite ideas is a morning wedding followed by a nice champagne brunch or even orange juice, for that matter.

Beverages end up being a tough issue. We've all been to those weddings with the open bar and maybe we've all enjoyed those weddings as well. However, an open bar is never a good idea. Yes, the reception is a celebration, and yes, we want our guests to enjoy themselves. However, we don't want people getting sick or even worse, getting a DUI because of our wedding. A great alternative to an open bar is providing some alcohol for free and then having a cash bar for the rest. Besides, if you are using a hotel or country club type place for the reception, you will not believe how much beer and wine costs. Since a keg of beer averages around $175 and a bottle of wine can be $30+, do the math and make a decision to limit the freebies. A tasteful way around it is to buy a keg and some champagne for a toast and leave the rest of the booze up to the discretion of your guests.

Another good reason to keep the free alcohol to a minimum is to keep your guests from embarrassing themselves and you. Toasts have been known to get ugly when given by inebriated people. Most people get nervous speaking in front of large groups but too much truth serum may end up in a disastrous confession or too much information on the bride or groom's past. Not a good scene at all. Another potential powder keg with the open keg is the tradition of getting the newlyweds to kiss on command. Especially if you require guests to "tell a story about the bride/groom" to get a kiss, you will want to make people pay for their own booze.

I don't even recommend allowing sober people to have an open microphone at an event like a wedding because there are many people in this world with too little tact and too big a mouth. Another thing I hate is the "sing a song with the word love in it" idea. If people who can't sing really need to make themselves look like idiots, they can find a karaoke bar. The only thing that really fits the situation is clinking the silver and china. It's classy and usually remains tasteful, so go with that.

One of the time-honored and most fun traditions of weddings is "the dance." I would say, find a way to do it inexpensively. I don't know about you, but I don't have any cousins in Pearl Jam and I didn't go to college with members of any bands who could play sober. So what are the options? Maybe you could have your parents find a band like Frankie Yankovic's Traveling Polka show or some Country Western cover band that specializes in sad songs. From my perspective, however, go with a DJ. They are much easier to find, usually much cheaper, and you have much more control. You can usually suggest certain songs and even if they play some bad rap song by mistake, you can go up and do requests and cut the tip. If giving musical freedom to someone you've never met frightens you, you can also self-produce.

I'm sure you have a friend or someone you know who has a really nice home sound system. What you can do is spend some time together as a couple picking out your favorite songs from your CD collection and ask friends for ones that you don't have. Before long, you can have a list of 50 to 60 songs that could easily fill four hours with your favorite music. From there, you can either make some tapes of your own or rope a friend into doing it for you. This is another good place for you as a man to take over and add real value. These tapes of your favorite music will be a really nice memory for you both and you will probably save a few hundred dollars. Nice.

One of the best reasons to have a dance and one of the few traditions that's actually functional and fun is the "Dollar Dance." This is the time when everyone gets in a line to pay actual money to dance with you. This is the only time in most people's lives when this will happen, so live it up! Also, it's a great way to get a chance to talk to a bunch of people one-on-one and make some extra money to use on the honeymoon!

One of the tackiest things to do at a reception is to play stripper music and do the garter toss. This event usually goes along with the bouquet toss but is really not tasteful and totally unnecessary. With the bouquet, most single women want to catch it so they will be next to get married. However, with the garter and single men, most guys actually put their hands in their pockets and hope that it doesn't land on their heads. So please skip it.

# 24

♦ ♦ ♦ ♦ ♦

## GIFT OPENING, OR HOW TO
## WASTE YOUR FRIENDS' TIME

I KNOW IT'S A TRADITION and your parents may tell you it's necessary. However, I'm here to help you say no. I'll even give you several good reasons and some ideas to replace the event with something even better.

First, most people have the rehearsal and dinner on Friday, wedding and reception on Saturday, and the gift opening on Sunday before they take off for the honeymoon. The idea to have another event on the day after the wedding, in my opinion, is overkill. No, that's not strong enough: In some cases, you are killing people. Yes, your wedding is fun and your friends and family are glad to be there, but enough is enough, for crying out loud. You already asked them to take Friday off, rent tuxes, buy gifts and travel to your wedding. Now you are going to try to make them watch you open gifts. Don't do it. Give them a break, let them use Sunday to unwind and travel home so the whole weekend isn't a total loss. Besides, no one except your parents and grandparents wants to watch you open your gifts anyway.

Another reason to cancel the gift opening is that it's another event for you or someone in your family to plan. Downsizing is key to keeping your sanity and this is a perfect place to cut. Also, you may want to save the gift opening for after the honeymoon and do it alone as husband and wife. It's a nice way to unwind after a trip and it's a lot of fun as well. Another benefit of doing this event alone is that you will get stupid stuff that you hate from somebody. If you are sitting in a room full of the people who gave you the stupid stuff, you have to fake your sincere pleasure. If you are alone with your new spouse, you can bond by openly mocking people who give you dumb things, which happens to be great fun.

One final thought. I'm not opposed to an event on the morning after the wedding, as long as you do it at a decent time so your guests who partied late and hard will be able to make it. Have a thank-you brunch or early lunch to thank everyone for helping out and show your appreciation for their attendance at the wedding. This is also a great way to spend more time with friends and relatives that come from far away whom you seldom get to see. Make it fun and short, but don't make anyone watch you open gifts. It's a crime.

# 25

◆ ◆ ◆ ◆ ◆

## OTHER PEOPLE'S WEDDINGS

*Ann and Bill were 23 and very excited for their wedding. As most young couples just out of college, they were ready for a party and so were all their friends. The "open" bar was stocked and ready to go and all their friends took advantage of this in a big way. One young man, let's call him Rolf, had the reputation (well deserved) of being the "wild thing." Needless to say, he tore it up and had a fabulous time at the reception. That wasn't the problem. Only later did Ann and Bill hear what happened after the reception. A group of revelers, including Rolf, went bar- hopping and came back to the hotel for some more fun. It was about 2:00 a.m., and Rolf decided to take his clothes off and hang his lower extremities out the hotel window. His room faced the pool and there were a few people out there, even at 2:00 a.m.*

*One of them happened to be his mother. Little did he know that as his mother was sipping her final cocktail of the evening with her two lady friends, she would glance up to see a naked man hanging out the window. Since she gave birth to and raised him, she recognized the butt (and the rest of his body) and was mortified. Needless to say, there were severe repercussions for this 23-year young man. After the wedding, Rolf checked himself (at the strong suggestion of Mom and others) into a treatment center and hasn't had a drink since. To this day, he drinks O'Doul's at parties. That wedding has become known by many as "the wedding that changed Rolf's life." The moral of the story: other people's weddings are usually boring but they could change your life. Also, keep your pants on.*

YOU MAY BE WONDERING WHY I'M WRITING THIS CHAPTER, but you won't have any question once you get into it. Have you been to any weddings of your ex-wives or girlfriends? This is like being invited to go to the dentist and being obligated to not only go and smile but also bring them a gift. In case you were wondering, I hate the dentist. Getting that hideous invitation in the mail that weighs about eight pounds is just about as frightening as getting a notice from the IRS that you are being audited, maybe even more so. Now don't get me wrong, and if I've been to your wedding, don't assume I hated it just because I'm writing this chapter. (Then again, you will never know.) Besides, I know there were people at my wedding who would have rather been seeing their urologist. I am okay with that; what comes around goes around. The important thing is being able to survive the inevitable: other people's weddings. I will hopefully be able to shed some light on that.

Anyway, weddings are usually fun events because you hopefully get a free meal and some booze and you get to mock other people's taste as well. However, there are also some problems but with a few suggestions, you can survive.

Summer weddings in small towns that are unbelievably far away from civilization and fun places you want to be are the worst. I mean seriously, what are people thinking when they get married in places like Podunk, Ohio? Just because the bride happens to be from some ridiculously small town in the middle of nowhere that's off the paved roads doesn't mean that you have to get married there. I grew up in a town with a population of 211. There is a church, a bar, and a community center and you can crawl between them, but there's no place to eat and no hotels and you can hardly even buy a tank of gas and a Coke for the road. Yes, your hometown may be quaint and swell and very romantic and if it means a lot to you to get married in a cornfield, then by all means go for it. Just please don't punish a bunch of people you hardly know by inviting them and pressuring them into coming.

Now, you might be saying, "Hey, if you're that opposed to attending other people's weddings, then just don't go." Great idea, but that's not entirely practical in most situations. Don't get me wrong, we've been invited to somewhere around 10,000 weddings in our young lives and have declined a few. I support the use of the "I regret I will be unable to attend" box on the RSVP card in a few situations. If the drive is longer than four hours or you have to fly and the only people you will know at the wedding are the bride and groom, forget it. If the wedding is on a holiday weekend, traffic will really suck and if you don't want to waste a long weekend by going to a wedding, please don't.

Yes, I know you may think I'm contradicting earlier advice to go ahead and have your weddings on holiday weekends if it works well for you. Again, the bride and groom are the most important people in the wedding. If holiday weekends work for them, that's fantastic but they shouldn't expect potential guests to be overjoyed about it. Another reason to decline attendance at other people's weddings includes the necessity of a vacation day from work. Yes, some people actually get married at like 2:00 on a Friday, which may again be great for them but it stinks for you (unless you hate your job like me and would love to leave early to see others get married).

I think we've properly established the need to say no to invitations if it's inconvenient or uncomfortable for you. Two quick pieces of advice that you will be required to follow are: let people know you're not coming and definitely send a gift. After going through the wedding process, there are a few things that I will remember for all time. One is the fact that I had to actually call people who I thought were moderately close friends to ask them if they were coming a week before my wedding. This really makes people angry when they are trying to come to final numbers for their caterer. Please return your regrets by phone or postcard or whatever as soon as you can. If not, the nice people who invited you may be paying $30 for a plate of food that will never get eaten.

Also, on a similar note, if for some reason you respond affirmatively and have something come up at the last minute, make sure you get word to the couple somehow. I screwed this up about a year after college. My insane girlfriend (not my wife) and I were on our way to some ridiculously small town for a wedding that neither of us wanted to go to. Very fun. Anyway, we got in a huge fight about two hours into the drive and broke up. Needless to say, she was crying and I was not so pleased either so we turned around and drove home. I think that couple is still pissed at me, and I'm so stupid that I never even wrote them a card or anything. In fact, I think I may have even returned their gift. Oops. Oh well, you can only have so many friends in life anyway. Besides, I think they are both doctors now and making millions so I wouldn't want to hang around them anyway.

So, please learn from my mistakes: Don't date insane women, please respond to invitations and lastly, send gifts. Just a couple quick notes on gifts. Some people have very expensive taste and register for crystal wine glasses and hand-painted china, both out of normal people's price range. It is exceedingly tacky to go in with others on gifts but do it anyway. For people who have enough money to buy really expensive gifts for someone they hardly know just because they're on the registry, please give the money to a food pantry in the name of the bride/groom instead.

I remember one time fresh out of college making a four-hour drive to a wedding with a bunch of friends. It was a bad scene because none of us had any money at the time. Six of us had to stay in the same hotel room and go in on one $100+ wine glass. Did we impress the bride? No, but we were able to eat and pay rent until we got real jobs. I've never known a single couple who has cross-referenced their invitation list with their gift list, but I'm sure it happens. In other words, getting a gift is not as big a deal as the RSVP, but it still shows that you know what you're doing and that's good occasionally.

◆ *Epilogue* ◆

To summarize, here are the Top 10 Quick Tips. Yes, I wish I had David Letterman's job. You could have just read these and squeaked by, but you really want your wedding to be the best so you'll be glad you didn't. However, everyone needs a cheat sheet, so here's yours:

1. Take a honeymoon right away; you will need it. If you have to, skimp on something else instead and do a honeymoon. Your guests won't remember the dinner, the music, or the cake, but you should never forget your honeymoon.

2. Do not, under penalty of death, hire a wedding coordinator/consultant. If you need one, you're overdoing it and you need to chill, relax, cut back, whatever.

3. Invite only people who you want. The guest list can get way out of hand, so pick a reasonable number that you can afford and stick to it. Don't invite distant relatives just because your mom says so, and don't invite people from work if you don't like them. Get over it. It's your wedding, not theirs.

4. Don't be engaged for longer than 12 months. Seriously, the longer you wait, the more difficult it will become to stick to your budget and original plan. We did the whole deal in nine months and it was fantastic.

5. Do not stress out about the members of your wedding party. If people will be disappointed about not being asked to buy an expensive dress or rent a tux to stand near you on your big day, they need to get a life. Pick who you want, not based on past performance, or the fact that you were in their wedding. Just pick the best people.

6. Set a budget early and stick to it. Also, even if you're getting a loan or scholarship from family, make it clear that you and your fiancée need to have 100% decision-making authority. If you can't get agreement on that, tell your family to keep their money and scale back so you can handle everything yourself. After all, money is the number one cause of divorce

in this modern world, and a wedding is a good place to start working together on it.

7. Pick a date that works best for you. If it has to be a holiday weekend, that's fine. It's your wedding. You're the ones getting married. If it's inconvenient for others, they don't have to be there. In most states you only need two witnesses!

8. Have fun! Make your big day the best one ever by working together. Be creative and put yourself into the planning of the event as a team. Customize the event by having it catered by your favorite restaurant, writing the vows yourselves, or having the ceremony outside in your favorite park. Just follow your hearts and it will be great.

9. Men are idiots + women are totally irrational = two strikes. Even if you're a man without a plan, spend time thinking of ways to add value any way you can. Try to get involved in management or administration, since you may not be able to pick out the best china or shoes that match the bridesmaids'dresses or flowers.

10. Marry the person you love and love them forever. This may sound a bit elementary, but the current odds tell us that 50% of all marriages end in divorce. Make sure you love the person you're marrying and if you don't know, don't get engaged or married. Also, love is a verb and it takes a lot of work so be prepared for the commitment you're making.

That's pretty much the deal. I honestly hope that you can move beyond being just "a man and *her* wedding" and that your work as a team is only the beginning of a happy marriage and fulfilling life.

◆ ◆ ◆

# ORDER FORM

A MAN *and*
*Her Wedding*
• • • •

To order copies of *A Man and Her Wedding*, please complete the information below. (Feel free to duplicate this form.)

I would like to order _____ copies of *A Man and Her Wedding* at $12.95 per copy (plus postage and handling).

Book Total
    ____copies at $12.95 per copy        $_____

Sales Tax
  Minnesota residents add 6.5%        $_____

Shipping and Handling
  $2 for first book, $1 for each
  additional book        $_____

Total amount enclosed        $_____

Checks should be made payable to: **Brant Creative**
Please do not send cash.

Ordered by:
Name: _____
Address: _____
City: _____
State: _____ Zip: _____
Phone: (____) _____

Shipped to (if different from above):
Name: _____
Address: _____
City: _____
State: _____ Zip: _____
Phone: (____) _____

Please complete this form and mail to:
**Brant Creative**
*4979 West End Lane*
*Minnetonka, MN 55345*
*email: sales@brantcreative.com*
*website: www.brantcreative.com*